DARK

DAYS

ALSO BY KATE ORMAND

The Wanderers
The Pack: The Sequel to The Wanderers

DARK DAYS

KATE ORMAND

Sky Pony Press
New York

Sky Pony Press books may be purchased in bulk at special discounts
for sales promotion, corporate gifts, fund-raising, or educational purposes.
Special editions can also be created to specifications. For details,
contact the Special Sales Department, Sky Pony Press,
307 West 36th Street, 11th Floor, New York, NY 10018
or info@skyhorsepublishing.com.

Sky Pony® is a registered trademark of Skyhorse Publishing, Inc.®,
a Delaware corporation.

Visit our website at www.skyponypress.com.

10 9 8 7 6 5 4 3 2 1

Library of Congress Cataloging-in-Publication Data

Ormand, Kate.
Dark days / Kate Ormand.
pages cm
Summary: "Sia only has fifteen more days to live before her sector is destroyed
by a cyborg army. But she decides to join a rebel group who are determined to
fight the cyborgs and live"—Provided by publisher.
Paperback ISBN: 978-1-5107-1710-7
EISBN: 978-1-62873-949-7
[1. Science fiction. 2. Cyborgs—Fiction. 3. Survival—Fiction.] I. Title.
PZ7.O63375Dar 2014
[Fic]—dc23
                                                        2013048798

Cover design by Kate Gartner

Printed in the United States of America

CONTENTS

For Andy, for everything

DARK

DAYS

15 DAYS

I wake to a shrieking sound.

The wailing surrounds me, echoing off the walls and interrupting fitful sleep filled with nightmares and torture.

I pat my hand on the nightstand until I find the alarm clock and make it stop. I rub my eyes. The red numbers on the clock display 6:03 a.m.

Red.

Red digital numbers, like the ones on the clock outside that towers above us all. Counting down, down, down. Red like blood, like rage, like hate, all of which surround me. I force myself to sit up and take a deep breath.

6:04 a.m. With not long to live, I don't want to spend any more time sleeping than necessary.

Yawning, I throw back the covers and fling my legs over the edge of the bed. I stretch, wiggling my fingers and toes in an overdramatic way, standing and reaching to the ceiling with arms that will hang cold and stiff from my shoulders in two weeks.

That's if they are still attached to my body.

I shudder and goose bumps flare up all over my skin. Some of the scenes aired on the Reports are horrific.

1

I do my best to block those images of mangled bodies and unidentifiable parts from my mind. And it makes me wonder if that makes me brave. I mean, that's why they're doing it, that's why they're showing us, isn't it? Is that what they're looking for, bravery?

Who knows.

I try not to torture myself with those kinds of questions; I have fifteen days to live, and I plan to make the most of them.

I slip into my desk chair. There's no school to go to anymore. There's no going out and meeting friends, no homework, no purpose to my life. The only things people care about now are how they look in front of the cameras, what they can do to prove their worth to the authorities, or how they can escape this place.

But there is no escape.

I open the desk drawer and pull out my notebook and pen. I've attempted to write a list of things I want to do before I die. I thought it would be a good idea. I thought it'd make me feel better. I also thought it'd be easier to do than it was. In the end I settled on four things.

1. *Swim in the lake.*

I want to swim in the sector's only lake. It's not very big and looks quite dirty, surrounded by overgrown grass with a thin layer of algae on top. It's the only place in the sector there is to swim, and I've seen people in it before. I've never been swimming and I don't know how to. But I'll figure it out.

2. *Climb the hill.*

The hill is beside the lake. The bushes are overgrown and the ground is a tangle of weeds and nettles. The thing is, I have never seen what's behind the metal walls that surround the sector. Never seen beyond the barriers that contain us, control us, trap us here. I know there is life beyond the wall. I've seen sector after sector on the Reports every day. They're just like ours, every one of them. Everything looks the same: the houses, the roads, the clock. The only difference is that the sectors I see on the TV screen are a wreck. They're splattered with blood and ash, and everyone's dead.

I guess our sector will look like that soon.

Climbing the hill is forbidden. And here, if you're told not to do something, you don't do it. But I don't care anymore. They're going to kill me anyway—what more can they do if I'm caught?

3. *Spend time with Mom and Dad.*

I want to spend at least an evening where we talk normal to one another. I want us to have ordinary conversations, laughing and joking as if none of this is happening. I want to sit with them and forget all the horror and the pain and the fear that's around us.

I'd considered crossing this one out, especially since the red digital numbers began their countdown on the clock tower. My mom's been glued to the Reports. She will not leave the living room. She will not open the blackout shutters that cover the windows. She will not speak to my dad

3

or me. I'm near giving up on number 3, but I want to give it one last chance before ruling it out completely.

   4.   Kiss a boy and fall in love.

I blush every time I read this one. It sounds so stupid, but I want to meet a boy. I want my first kiss, and I want to fall in love. But nobody can meet someone and fall in love in fifteen days, right? I swipe the pen across the paper, putting a thick black line through the second half of the sentence.

It's all kind of pathetic, really, but I guess that's what happens when you know you're going to die. You stop taking little things for granted and try to figure out what you want to do in the time you have left. Unfortunately, I'm very limited to what I *can* do here. But this list gives me purpose, something to strive for, a distraction, because I refuse to let myself spend the rest of my days fearing my death and mourning my short life.

Gliding my eyes down the list a final time, I decide that today I'll attempt number 3. I figure things will only get worse with my mom the longer I avoid her. With a determined nod, I close the notebook and shove it back into the drawer.

After taking a quick shower, I blast my hair with the dryer. I pace around my room as far as the wire will allow, hunting on the floor for something to wear. I get dressed in whatever I pick up first—black jeans, a gray T-shirt, and a black jacket—and head downstairs to find my parents.

Mom and Dad have reacted in incredibly different ways since the announcement on the Reports. We all have. Dad's fairly quiet and I have no idea how he's feeling inside, but he keeps a brave face. I hardly see him anymore, though. Mom is a wreck. I guess I can't blame her. It's hard to believe that this is actually happening sometimes. Other times the reality of it hits me so hard I can't breathe.

As I descend the stairs two at a time, the first thing I hear is the television airing the Reports. The second is my mom's muffled cries. I take a deep breath and walk toward the living room.

I push the door open and take a step inside. The room is small and stuffy. The walls are bare and painted a murky olive green, quite like the color of the water in the lake. The color of the walls darkens the room and makes the space appear smaller than it actually is, which is only made worse by the blackout shutters. Walking into the living room fills me with a sense of being underground.

It takes my eyes a moment to adjust, as the only light source is the flickering television screen. Filling up the rest of the space is a worn coffee table, an ancient floor lamp, one brown armchair, and a sofa that isn't quite the same shade as the chair, though it could have been once. Everyone in the sector has the exact same living room: same furniture, same layout, same color.

Dad and I don't come into this room anymore except to check on Mom. She won't move from the sofa; she's spent days and days huddled up in a nest of cushions in the dark. We've never been close, but she's still my mom and this isn't what I want for her. I've tried to help her, but she doesn't respond to anything I say or do. I just wish she'd stop watching the Reports, watching the gruesome after-math of every attack and imagining what it'll be like when it happens to us.

Right now, Mom is lying on the sofa, her face pressed into a pillow while she sobs. The screen captures my attention. The Reports are showing the latest sector to have fallen. Cameras line the streets of each sector and the Reports air the recordings with a voice-over. The zero displayed on the clock tower on the screen is scorching red—final. I see walls crumbling, houses on fire, dead bodies, and blood and ash coating the floors and walls. I see body parts and building rubble scattered in the streets. We never get to see what did it, though. The cyborgs are left to our imagination.

I wonder if I'll be scared when the time comes.

I tear my eyes away from images I see too often on that screen and look for the remote. Mom has her hand curled around it. I attempt to take it from her, but she screams at me. "NO!"

I jump back, startled. She hasn't said even a word to me in days. I don't respond at first, I can't. I tug again at the remote.

"I said *no*," she says. Three words.

I shake my head. "Why do you watch this?" I ask, desperate to know. "Why do you torture yourself?"

I hold my breath, waiting for her to speak to me again. Still clutching the remote, she pulls herself upright and wipes her puffy, bloodshot eyes with the sleeve of my dad's shirt. She's been wearing the same clothes for days: Dad's shirt and a pair of old, baggy yoga pants. Her feet are bare and I smelled them when I walked into the room.

She's stopped washing, sleeping, and eating. She drifts off sometimes, when she can't help it. But she always has nightmares from spending every waking moment drilling the images from the Reports into her head. When she sleeps I can hear her screaming and thrashing. Then she wakes up and it stops, and I only hear her crying softly. It's horrible and I hate the authorities for doing this to us. For stringing it out and watching us suffer.

"Mom?" I say, stepping closer and bending down slightly to come into her line of vision, blocking the television screen.

She can barely keep her eyes open. Their shade of brown is so dark it blends with her pupils. I used to think her eyes were amazing. They are the same color as mine. They used to be so big and striking; now they just look like deep black holes of utter misery. There are dark-purple, gloomy shadows smudged beneath them, too. And her short hair, as black as mine, is thick with grease and matted with knots.

I hold back tears. I promised myself that I would not cry, that I would not spend any of the time I have left feeling miserable. Mom stares at me, looking years older than she had nine days ago, back before we found out what was going to happen to us.

"I watch it," she says, through gritted teeth, "because I *need* to know what will happen."

"But why? Can't you forget it? Can't you turn the television off and enjoy the rest of your life?" I argue.

She spits out a vicious laugh. "What's to enjoy? You want me to live like you and your father, you mean? Is that it?"

She stares at me with wide, wild eyes.

"Oh," she continues, "I am sorry that being ripped to pieces, or burnt alive, or crushed to death bothers me—" I put my hand up to stop her. I shudder at the effect her words have on me. I don't watch the Reports for a reason.

I want to leave the room, but at the same time I crave to hear her voice, now that she's finally speaking.

"Where's Dad?" I ask, but it's useless. She merely shrugs and repositions herself so that she can see past me to the TV. Silent tears run down her cheeks as her unblinking eyes stare vacantly at the scenes being aired.

I don't look at the screen again, but I still hear the sound of the chaos—buildings groaning as they collapse, fires blazing and crackling—and the running commentary from the female voice-over.

I finally give up and leave to see if Dad is home. I want to tell him that Mom spoke to me. But just as I cross through the doorway, she speaks again.

"It didn't used to be like this."

I spin around to face her. She isn't looking at me, though. Her eyes are still on the screen. For a moment I wonder if I imagined hearing her speak.

"What did you say?" I ask, even though I know. I just want to hear her voice again.

"It never used to be like this, here in the sector," she whispers.

"What do you mean? What was it like?" I say. She's speaking so softly that I can hardly hear her, so I place myself on the edge of the sofa, leaning in a little to listen.

"I'm afraid, Sia."

"I know you are," I say soothingly. "We all are. It's okay to be."

"You were just a baby," she says. "You won't remember."

"Remember what?" I ask. She is making no sense, but I'm careful not to push too hard.

"You won't remember. You were just my baby girl when the walls went up around us and sealed us here in the sector." She reaches out and strokes the side of my face. It is the most affection she's shown me in a long time, even before all of this. I try not to flinch at her touch. She then takes my hand in both of hers and grips it tightly.

I don't remember the walls going up, but I do know what it was like before. It's no secret. We were taught the history of the sector in school. It wasn't much different than how it is now. The biggest thing to change was the introduction of the walls and a midnight curfew. We're locked in our houses from twelve until six. Anyone caught out on the streets is punished. Rules aren't made to be broken.

"Is that what you mean? It didn't used to be like this because there were no walls?"

"They said keeping us contained would keep us safe. But look at us now. We're trapped. The walls were meant to shield us from harm, but now we'll die because we can't get out. We're like animals in a cage. Look," she says, taking one hand from mine to point at the television. "Look what is going to happen to us because of those walls and the people who put them there."

I don't look.

"Sia, look what is going to happen to us!" she says angrily. Using her free hand, she grabs my face. Her long, filthy nails dig into my skin. I shriek and try to shake my head free of her grasp. I yank my hand from hers and bat her away, but despite being so malnourished, she holds on tight. She forces my head around to face the screen.

"I don't want to see!" I cry, squeezing my eyes shut.

"You have to! I'm trying to explain it to you," she demands.

I stand up, forcing her to let go of me.

She stands up too, tears pouring from her eyes, and takes a step toward me. Her legs shake, her feet unsteady on the floor. Knees buckling, she falls to the ground in a heap and sobs hysterically.

My throat tightens, and I blink away tears.

I try to help her up, but as soon as I put one hand on her, she lashes out and hits it away. She curls up, with her head in her hands. Her cries are loud, her words muffled and undecipherable.

"Mom, let me help you," I say.

She continues to cry and shakes her head. I move behind her and wrap my arms around her waist, pulling her up again and trying to get her back over to the sofa.

I can feel her ribs beneath a thin layer of skin. Dad and I make food for her, but she hardly touches it.

Struggling between my arms, her cries worsen.

"Mom, stop, *please*. Let me help."

"You can't help me," she wails. "You can't help me." She can hardly catch her breath when I finally sit her back on the sofa. "I hate this, Sia. I hate this so much."

"I know. I do too. What can I do? I want to help you."

"I don't want to be here. I don't want to die like that." She points at the screen again, tears dripping from the end of her chin. Her face is red and blotchy.

"Neither do I, but we can't get out."

"We have to find a way, we *have* to." She reaches out and clutches my arm, her wild eyes bore into mine with desperation. "We have to find a way to get out. I can't die like that. I can't."

"Mom, please! There isn't a way. I'm sorry. There just isn't."

She screams—a piercing sound that shakes my bones. I stumble backward, banging my legs against the coffee table. Then I dart out of the room, away from her, slamming the door behind me.

She doesn't follow.

Sitting halfway up the stairs, I hear her whimpering quietly. I rub my throbbing jaw, feeling the crescent-shaped marks her nails have left on my skin. I don't cry, even though I easily could.

Mom blames the walls for what is happening to us, but I know it is much more than that. They're just an obstacle that stops us from getting away and saving ourselves. It is ironic, really, considering they were put there to protect us in the first place. Or so we were told in class.

I think about what they'll teach in history classes in the New World when all of this is over. I'm guessing they'll start where we do—climate change and the reduction of the population and extinction of most of the world's species. Then they'll discuss how the people were spread out on what was left of the planet. And then how the sectors came about, to round everyone up and create communities where people could stay together, stay safe.

No one really knows what's outside the sectors anymore—they call it the Rough. Rumors suggest that there are some people still out there; some people they missed. I call them strays. Most call them savages.

The class will go on to learn that people's lives were considered precious at that time. So after a while, they were walled in and "protected."

That's what we were taught.

Now for the new part—what will be taught after all the sectors are destroyed. I imagine most of the class won't be listening anymore—doodling in their textbooks or looking out the window. But the teacher will go on anyway, discussing how the authorities murdered many of the citizens in the walled sectors, cutting the population down even more. Then the remaining people inhabited the New World.

It's crazy to chop the population down more when we've already lost billions in the last eighty years. But numbers aren't their concern—quality is. The New World wants to start afresh: rebuild the world and do it better. They want to start again, take control, and make this world the very best that it can be.

"So, class," I imagine the New World history teacher saying. "Selection to find the best people to populate the New World began, and all the useless humans that weren't good enough to live here were slaughtered brutally and unfairly and—" I stop myself. I need to get out of this house.

When I enter the kitchen there is a small scrap of paper stuck to the fridge door—from Dad. Annoyingly, all that's written on there is *gone out,* which I could have figured out without the note. I must have just missed him.

I open the fridge door and the stench of sour milk assaults my nostrils. Using one hand to hold my nose and the other to remove the carton, I shut the fridge with my hip and pour the curdled milk down the sink.

The kitchen is small and dark, and again, exactly the same as all kitchens in our sector. Off-white shelves line the dreary, beige walls. Counters and cupboards in the same color stretch around the sides, only breaking their pattern for the stove, fridge, and sink. And a small round table, surrounded by four wooden chairs, sits in the middle of the room, taking up most of the floor space. Still, I like it better than the living room.

I notice that the shelves are low on food. I open some of the cabinets, finding them just as bare. So I head back upstairs to borrow Dad's money-card. I take Mom's too, just in case Dad doesn't have enough money left on his to buy food.

I don't have a money-card of my own yet. Everyone in the sector is assigned one once they finish their education at eighteen and start working. Everyone receives the same payment on their money-cards, no matter their jobs. We're all matched with the career we're predicted best at, then paid each week. I think I would have been in one of the factories. Dad works maintenance in one, and Mom's a packer of medical supplies. With this system, I've never thought of any person, any family, as better than any other. We're all treated the same. We aren't individual. We're equal.

I guess I was wrong.

As I make my way to the sector's only food store, I start to wonder what I'll miss most about this place. Sure, there isn't much to it. There is no color, no vibrancy, no energy. Just streets lined with dull, block houses in tidy rows, perfectly parallel to one another. Roads turn at sharp angles, with each corner made complete by a chunky black camera with a red blinking light to let you know you are being watched.

There are no trees, so I never get to see any birds in their nests or watch the leaves transform from green to orange to brown, only to fall off and crumble to nothing then start all over again.

There is no grass, other than the small trimmed patches outside each house, big enough for only two people to sit on. I guess you could count the wild grass by the lake and the hill too, but it's filled with bugs and nettles.

There is nothing particularly pretty about the sector, nothing you can really enjoy. I like to watch the sky, though. I like to see fluffy clouds drift overhead during the day. And the stars that occupy the night sky.

It's spring here, I think. But there's a sharp chill in the air that's lingered since winter. It never quite warms, not really. But it is home, and it is familiar.

The sun is climbing up into the sky, and the rows of packed houses cast shadows along the sidewalks. I walk in the middle of the road, where the shadows can't reach, enjoying the feel of the early morning sun on my skin.

When I round a corner, I hear a clanging noise, metal on metal. Following the sound, I find a group of people hitting the wall with shovels and anything else they think might break through it. Don't they realize that people have tried this before? Don't they know that others have done all they can to get out—and died trying? There isn't even a dent in the wall. Not a scratch or mark left by their efforts. I walk by them without stopping, noticing the cameras on the buildings beside me slowly swivel to face the group, the red light blinking, watching.

When I pass my best friend Kyra's house, I slow down in case I see her. I'm supposed to meet her here tomorrow, and I know I wouldn't be welcome dropping by unannounced. It'd be nice to see her face today, though. Especially as the only person I've spoken to is Mom.

I stop in front of the house. Kick at some loose stones with the tip of my scuffed boot.

Kyra's dad, framed by the upstairs window, looks down at me. He doesn't look pleased to see me. I should leave. Instead, I raise my hand tentatively. Offer a half-smile. He shakes his head, slowly.

A warning?

He's warning me away. I'm allowed to visit them tomorrow, not today. I should go. And this time I do.

I reach the center of the sector, where the clock tower and all the public buildings are situated. Aside from the factories, the food store is the largest building in the sector. Even so, it isn't an impressive building. The walls are a smooth, dull gray, like everything else. There are no windows, just flat walls.

There are glass double doors on the left signposted ENTRANCE and glass double doors on the right signposted EXIT. The signs above the doors stand out with red painted letters, adding some color to the otherwise muted structure. The sign above the store is red, too. It is lit up, though some of the letters have burned-out bulbs.

I grab one of the shopping carts rolling around in the wind outside the entrance and stroll inside.

It's quiet.

I look up at the ceiling—a zigzag of structures holding in place a corrugated metal roof—where the fluorescent tube lights cut out and flicker back on again. I can hear them buzzing in the silence.

The shelves are almost bare. We haven't had a delivery, and I'm guessing we won't be getting one. As I enter the

16

first aisle, I'm surprised by the mess I find. Jars are spinning on the floor, some broken.

Loud shouting echoes around the stripped shelves. It sounds like a fight. I peer around a corner and see two men wrestling on the ground. There's a woman with one arm around a crying baby and the other clutching a burst box of cereal. The men are fighting over the food.

I hadn't realized how bad things had gotten. I hadn't realized that simply stepping out of my house puts me in danger.

I almost bolt from the store and abandon everything. Then I consider that I might not get a chance to come back. In fact, I know I won't. I decide to risk it while I'm here and fill my shopping cart with whatever I can. As fast as I can.

I rack my brain over what's most important, but I can't think logically in my panic. I run up and down the aisles, grabbing at anything, hardly glancing at what I am picking up. The shopping cart gets heavier and harder to push and I decide I'm done. I head for the doors, but there's a boy at the checkout counter wearing a staff uniform.

I toy with the idea of running, but I'm not a thief, and I'd brought the money-cards with me assuming I'd have to pay. I just want to get out of here. I look at the doors and back at the boy, then make my way over to the counter.

As I get closer I realize he's not much older than me. Maybe eighteen. In normal circumstances, I'd have been happy to go over to his checkout.

The first thing I notice about him is his tattoos: they start at his wrists and work their way up his strong arms, covering every bit of skin until the pattern is cut off at the tips of his T-shirt sleeves.

The second thing I notice is his dark-brown hair shaped around his face. His eyes are dark too, like my mom's, but they hold life and energy, rather than misery and pain. And they're watching me as I approach.

Despite his good looks and the way he watches me, the very sight of him standing behind the counter irritates me. I don't want to stop. I don't want to talk. I want to get out of here and go home where I'm safe. Safe for fifteen days, anyway.

I stop and unload the shopping cart for the boy to scan and pack up.

"What are you doing?" he asks.

His question surprises me. Isn't the answer obvious? "Um . . . paying?" I reply.

"Why?" he says. He hasn't scanned anything yet.

"That's what you do in stores."

He stares at me, eyebrows furrowed. "Nobody else has paid for anything," he tells me. "They snatched whatever they could carry and took off."

"Maybe you should quit," I say with a smirk. "Are you going to scan these? I don't want to stay here for long."

"Are you here alone?" he asks, ignoring my question and still not picking up anything to scan.

"Yes. Can you start scanning?" I say, pointing to the food.

18

"What?" he says, glancing down like he's only just noticed I've put things in front of him. "Oh, you can go ahead and take those."

I stare at him. "Are you sure?"

"Yeah, go ahead," he says, and starts throwing items back into the shopping cart. I join him in loading it back up. "Do you watch the Reports?" he asks while we work. It's a strange question. No one really talks about the Reports.

"No," I tell him. "Not if I can help it."

"Do you know who Damien Hoist is?"

I grit my teeth. "*Yes.*"

"So you know what's happening?"

"Of course I do!"

"Right, yeah. Of course," he says, rubbing the back of his neck. "So, are you afraid?"

Suddenly I wonder if he's here from the New World and this is an interview. I wonder if I say the right things and act brave, he'll offer my family and me a place in the New World. "No, I'm not scared," I say confidently, standing up a little straighter.

He tilts his head, considers me. "I'm Mace, by the way," he says.

I narrow my eyes. "Sia," I say.

"I'll walk you home, Sia. You could get jumped on your own with a cart full of food. People are stocking up to go into hiding until the machines move on."

So he's not from the New World. My shoulders slump, disappointed. "Do you think that'll work?" I ask. "Hiding until they're gone?" If only it was that simple.

"No one has survived an attack in any of the other sectors. I think they're kidding themselves. But I suppose it gives them hope."

"I guess. But I'm not sure whether that's a good thing."

We walk slowly together. He pushes the shopping cart for me. I look at him out of the corner of my eye, wondering why he's still working at the store in the state it's in. My eyes run over his name tag and I stop.

"Kline?" I say, then watch his eyes dip down and rest on the tag.

"Oh. Busted," he says with a short laugh. I cross my arms over my chest, trying to act tough. I'm suddenly leery of the boy who lied about his name.

"So, which is it?" I ask, attempting to keep fear absent in my tone. I edge closer to the shopping cart, readying myself to grab it and run. My family needs this food and I'm not willing to make another trip to the store. I'm not letting this guy take it from me.

"It's Mace," he says. "I didn't lie about my name." He rips the name tag off his T-shirt, nipping a tiny hole in the fabric.

I launch forward and push him using all the strength I have. I think the shock of my hit, more than the impact of it, is what makes him release his hold on the cart. In one swift movement, I grab the handle and start running, not once looking back at Mace. Or Kline. Whoever he is.

"Sia! Wait!" he calls after me.

I hear his feet slapping against the concrete. I force myself to go on, will my legs to go faster and the wheels of the shopping cart to spin quicker.

"Sia!" he yells again. I still don't look back. I still don't slow down.

There's no one on the streets. It's unusually quiet for this time of day. I spare a glance at the clock tower. The numbers are still the same. So where is everybody? Hiding already?

As if in answer to my question, a man appears from an alley between houses and wraps his arms around my waist. A scream escapes my lips as he tackles me to the ground. I hit my chin on the hard pavement, causing me to bite my tongue and draw blood.

The man's grip loosens and two pairs of legs fill my slanted vision. Two men are stealing my supplies.

Everything that comes next happens so fast. Shots are fired. I flinch and cover my head. Then the two men scurry back to the alley they came from like rats. Items fall from their hands as they run.

I sit up and spit blood from my mouth, repulsed by the coppery taste. *Shots, I heard gunshots.* Afraid, I search for the source. Will I be shot now that this new person has come to steal my food?

But no one else is here, only Mace.

He picks everything up that's fallen from the shopping cart, and from the arms of the two men, and throws it back into the cart. So he faked being a checkout boy *and* he carries a gun? Everything about him screams trouble.

Mace approaches me and holds out his hand to help me up. Without taking it, I get myself to my feet. He laughs.

"Come here," he says, reaching out to touch my face.

21

I step back. "Don't touch me. I mean it." He might have saved me, but that's not to say I trust him. "You're not getting my food," I say.

"Sia, I'm not trying to take anything from you. I'm trying to help you."

I stare at him. "Where is everyone?" I whisper.

Mace shrugs. "People are handling the news in different ways." *Don't I know it*, I think, with Mom and Dad in mind. "You shouldn't be on your own. It's not safe."

I glare at him. "I just want to go home."

"I'll take you, just don't hit me again. And let me check your face."

I reach up and wince when I touch my grazed chin. Mace takes a cautious step toward me. He takes my face in both his hands and gently tilts my head upward.

"That'll be okay," he says, releasing me. "Just clean it up when you get home."

We walk the short distance to my house in silence. I'm still not sure what I think of him pretending to be someone he isn't. And it worries me that he carries a gun. No one needs a gun in the sector. I've never seen one before, never even heard of anyone owning one.

I slow to a stop as we reach my house and turn to face him. "Thank you," I say quietly.

"Don't mention it."

I clear my throat. "And, um, sorry for, you know, pushing you." I feel my cheeks heat up.

Mace smiles. "You've got a mean swing."

"Yeah, right."

"No, really. You scared me back there," he says, still smirking.

I push him playfully, then catch myself. What am I doing? I turn my back to him and end the conversation, walking up the path to the front door.

"Sia, wait," Mace says.

I don't turn around.

"Sia, please. Can we start again?"

"Start what again?" I ask. "There's nothing to start."

"I made a bad first impression." I blow out a puff of air. He's got that right. "Look, I'll explain everything if you meet me tomorrow."

I don't speak and turn away from him again. I'm afraid that I'll say yes. He runs up the path until he's beside me. I quicken my pace but he grabs the shopping cart. "You know, you're not supposed to take these," he says.

I cluck my tongue. "You're trespassing, you know."

"Just take this," he says. He scribbles on a piece of paper and thrusts it toward me.

"If I do will you go away?" I say.

"Yes. If you take it and promise to read it then I'll go away." I take the piece of paper. "Don't show anyone else," he says, then releases the cart. "I'll see you tomorrow."

I turn around to tell him he won't, but he's already walking away.

14 DAYS

6:00 a.m.

I drag myself out from beneath the warm covers of my bed. There's blood on my pillow. I feel groggy, and I'm aching all over.

The attack on the way home yesterday has really taken effect. My muscles are stiff, my chin is scabbed and sore, still splitting and bleeding when I move my jaw. But what is affecting me most—more than any injury or shock—is Mace. I haven't looked at the piece of paper he gave me. I was too shaken last night to handle any more surprises.

I hear a click as curfew is lifted and the shutters are unlocked. They open and pale morning light floods into the room.

I slump into my desk chair and pull open the top drawer. Mace's note is resting on top of my notepad, but I still don't want to read it. Not yet. Not today. I pull out the notepad from beneath it and let the tatty piece of paper fall deeper into the drawer. I'm not meeting him today—nothing will change that—so there's no point in looking.

I'm going to see my best friend, Kyra, for the second to last time before we die. Today is about her, not Mace.

I flip open the notebook and look at my list again. Nothing to tick off. I feel lousy, like I wasted a whole day yesterday. All I did, after dumping the shopping on the kitchen table, was grab a snack bar and shut myself in my room. Away from Mom, who was still watching the Reports when I returned. Away from Dad, which was easy because he was nowhere in sight. Again.

I don't know where Dad's going or what he's doing. I wish I could spend a little more time with him before the end, but I won't force it. I plan to distance myself from him and Mom in the final days, anyway. I don't want to be near them when it happens. I don't want to see them die, and I don't want them to see me die, either.

I place the tip of the pen against the paper next to number 3. Ink smudges around the nib. I hesitate, then drag the pen across *Spend time with Mom and Dad.*

I hover over number 4 and think of Mace again.

No. I catch myself. Mace is not *that* boy. I don't know who is, but it's not him. Not the boy with a false name and a gun.

Then why can't I stop thinking about him?

I open the drawer to put the notebook back, catching sight of the letter again. *Today is about Kyra,* I remind myself, and close the drawer.

Since the new Reports started, and we found out that we were all going to die, Kyra has mostly been at home with her family. Her dad is really strict, always has been, and he decided that their remaining time will be spent together and with no one that isn't a relative. They've completely shut themselves off, and I haven't had much chance to speak to Kyra about it. She begged and pleaded with her dad for him to let her see me. In the end he agreed to once this week and once next. Next week will be the last time we ever see each other. A lump forms in my throat and I'm quick to swallow it back down. I want to enjoy today.

Kyra's mom and dad won't let her leave the house to meet me, so I'm going over there at 10:00 a.m. I wonder if they'll make us stay in the same room as them, or whether we'll be granted some privacy and be able to sit in Kyra's bedroom. I want to ask her how she feels and how her family is coping. I want to tell her about yesterday, about the store, about the attack. And maybe about Mace.

I still have a little time to spare before leaving, so I go to the kitchen to eat breakfast.

There is a scrap of paper stuck to the fridge. The same one as yesterday, flipped over with a new note. This one reads: *Sia, we need to talk this afternoon.* My stomach lurches. I don't want a serious talk. I hate serious talks, and this sounds like a serious talk to me.

I start to panic and run through what it could possibly be about in my head. I quickly force myself to stop, to put it out of my mind. Nothing will spoil my morning with Kyra.

I've suddenly lost my appetite, but I make a small bowl of oatmeal anyway. I eat it quickly. It burns my tongue—I don't allow it time to cool—but I'm too wound up to care.

Everyone's interfering with how I want to spend my time. I can't see Kyra as much as I want to when it matters the most. My dad keeps his distance when it suits him, then springs this talk on me out of the blue. My mom's getting worse by the day, glued to the Reports.

And then there's Mace and his annoying ability to creep into my mind when I don't want him there. He's a stranger! Why am I so drawn to him?

"Bye, Mom," I call, out of habit, as I grab my battered boots from beside the door. We haven't spoken since our fight yesterday.

Outside, I take a deep breath and click the door shut without waiting for her reply. It's a reply that won't come.

Each day I feel more and more claustrophobic inside that house. Suffocated by those four walls. Things are getting worse, as is to be expected, but I hadn't taken into account how difficult it would be to live with Mom's constant misery and Dad's unexplained absences. It worries me that all of this will affect the way I want to live the last days of my life.

After all, it is *my* life.

I know they're my parents and I should love them, which I do, and be there for them, which I am. But these are my last days, and I can't live them for someone else. They're not exactly living their lives for me anymore.

I set off for Kyra's, taking in the familiar scenery of the sector. Boring gray house after boring gray house. The only buildings that are different—and only in size, rather than appearance—are the public buildings, like the stores, the computer library, the factories, and the school.

We'd been excused from school that day—that day we found out what is going to happen to us. Only, we didn't know what was actually going on until we got home. The teachers left it to parents to explain to their children. Everyone wanted to handle it differently, I suppose.

So class was dismissed for unknown reasons. We ran down the corridors and through the heavy metal gates as fast as our legs would go. I'm fast, so I was one of the first out, dragging a panting Kyra along behind me through the flow of bodies.

Most students, like Kyra and me, didn't go home right away. We spent the day wandering around the sector together. It was a nice day. The sun was out, even if the breeze was a little chilly. It felt too good to be true, spending a school day out of school with my best friend. It was a great day until I got home.

Then I found out what was really happening, and it quickly became the darkest day of my life (so far). Mom couldn't tell me. She locked herself upstairs in the bathroom so it was Dad who had to pick up the pieces, as usual. He told me straight, told me everything, then held me while I cried.

That morning there had been a Report aired on the television. It was timed during recess at school and was mandatory for all adults to watch. The Report showed them a new place—an advanced sector. I wanted to see it myself.

At first, I thought it was great. I thought the sectors were getting an upgrade or something. I thought we'd no longer live in such a boring place or that we wouldn't be so restricted anymore. I had so many questions, so many visions of what it would be like.

Dad explained what was really going to happen, though. He said that the New World was incredibly selective and that not all of us would be chosen to move there. I was disappointed that I might not get the chance to go, but still excited and interested to hear about it.

Then he told me the worst part. The part that shattered me. The part that made me feel as though I'd been kicked in the stomach and had the wind knocked out of me.

He told me that those who aren't chosen will be slaughtered by an army.

A cyborg army.

"You've got one hour," Mr. Foxe warns me.

"Yes, sir," I reply politely. He glares at me for a moment before stepping aside to let me into the house. He's changed a lot since I saw him last. Don't get me wrong, he's always been grumpy and unpleasant—it's his appearance that's changed, not his personality. Noticeable worry wrinkles wear deep around his eyes and across his forehead. Dark shading surrounds his eyes, making them tiny when he glares at me.

"KY!" he yells, his mouth inches from my ear. I wince and take another step away from him.

Kyra comes bounding down the stairs and I'm relieved to see her. She throws her arms around me. She's tall, like her dad, and has to stoop to hug me.

"Sia! I'm so glad to see you!" she mumbles against my hair.

I feel Mr. Foxe's presence behind me, watching our exchange.

"Um, thanks," I say quietly. "It's good to see you, too."

"Come on," Kyra says, grabbing my hand and pulling me up the stairs with her.

"Fifty-seven minutes, girls," Mr. Foxe calls up after us, and I have no doubt that in exactly fifty-seven minutes, he'll be up here ready to escort me out. He'll probably throw me out if he has to.

Once we're in Kyra's bedroom, she closes the door and pulls me into another hug.

"I've missed you so much, Sia," she says, obvious pain in her voice. I feel it, too. "It's been hell locked up in the house all day every day." She lets go. I see her eyes are filled with tears. Mine heat up too, but I blink them away.

We sit together on her twin bed, legs crossed, facing each other. Her curly brown hair, which usually falls haphazardly around her heart-shaped face, is pulled back into a bushy ponytail. She's wearing yoga pants and a baggy, knit sweater with sleeves that cover her hands. It's odd to see her dressing like this; Kyra nearly always wears dresses and cardigans. I'm the one who wears baggy sweaters and dark jeans stuffed into my scruffy black boots.

"How are things at your house?" she asks me in a broken voice.

"Pretty bad," I admit. "Dad's never around, and Mom's not really herself. Well, I mean, she is, but a worse version

31

of herself. I don't know how to explain it. She won't stop watching the Reports."

Kyra shivers. "Have you seen them?" she whispers. I nod and her eyes widen. "Dad won't let me."

"Good," I say. "You don't want to see."

"Is it that bad?" she asks, and tears start rolling down her cheeks.

"Let's not talk about them," I say. I don't want to lie to her, but I don't want to tell her what I've seen. "What's been going on here?"

"My dad can't understand why we haven't been chosen to leave here, with him being a good doctor and all. He thinks the authorities are still watching us. That's why he's being so weird about you coming over here." She looks at me guiltily. "Sorry, I didn't mean that."

"No, it's fine," I say. "I know we won't be chosen. I understand why your dad doesn't want to be seen mixing with us."

"Sia, don't be offended. You know what he's like."

"I do. It's fine."

"It's just, we keep seeing families go from here and hoping it'll be us next. But as it gets closer to the end, Dad's starting to think we won't be picked. Do you think there's no hope left at this stage?"

"There's still two weeks to go. Plenty of time," I say.

"Sorry, Sia. I shouldn't be talking like this—about saving my family and myself when you're going to be here when the machines come. Do you know what you're going to do?"

"What do you mean? There's nothing I can do."

"You could hide."

I shrug. "I don't think it'll be that easy."

"Well, you have to do something! You can't just stand around and wait to die."

I feel sick. All of this wondering and waiting hasn't been an issue in our house. I always knew, from that day, that my family would never be picked to leave. I knew we'd die here, along with the other people who were deemed unworthy to live. Mom and Dad's jobs are too ordinary. As a family, we're too ordinary. There's nothing that makes us stand out. No special skills. No spark. Nothing that makes us better than anyone else. I thought Kyra and her family might stand a chance, but people have been being saved for a week now. As the clock gets closer to zero, the chances are becoming less and less likely that others will be spared.

"I can't do anything," I whisper. "The only escape is being chosen by the authorities. Everyone wants it. Everyone envies those who are picked. Not everyone can go, though."

I take a deep, shaky breath and look up at Kyra. She's staring at me. Wow, this isn't fun at all.

"This is bad, right?" she says. "Like, really, really bad."

I nod. "I'm just trying to make the most of what time I have left," I tell her. Kyra's eyes fill up again. More tears.

The door opens. Mr. Foxe peeks in to tell us how long we have left. I cluck my tongue at the annoyance of his presence. He cuts off mid-sentence when he sees Kyra crying in front of me. Something tells me I won't be getting the rest of my time with her.

"What's going on here?" Mr. Foxe barks. I look back at Kyra. She's crying harder now, her face in her hands.

"Nothing," I say pathetically. "Kyra's just upset like everyone else."

Kyra's mom appears in the doorway, peering over Mr. Foxe's shoulder with swollen red eyes.

Great.

She gasps when she sees us and slips around Kyra's dad to get to her daughter. She crashes down onto the bed beside Kyra and wraps an arm around her, brushing loose hair back from her face. Mrs. Foxe is a petite woman with a tiny frame. Stood back-to-back, the tip of Mrs. Foxe's head would only just reach Kyra's shoulders. She was always really healthy, bustling around with mountains of energy. She's now slightly hunched, drained-looking. It's then that I realize Kyra's family is falling apart, just like mine.

"I think you've seen enough of each other for today," Mr. Foxe says. Mrs. Foxe doesn't even look at me. "Kyra will be in contact regarding next week. Though I may have to reconsider if this is the effect you have on my daughter."

I sigh and stand up. "Bye, Kyra," I say. "Mrs. Foxe." But neither looks up at me; both are still locked in an embrace and crying all over each other. I shake my head. Something about the way they're reacting annoys me. I'm suddenly glad to leave.

Once I step out of the house, Mr. Foxe expresses his annoyance with a forceful slam of the front door. I close my eyes. *It's fine*, I tell myself. It's fine. I don't care how many doors Mr. Foxe slams, or how many tears Mrs. Foxe sheds; it's them making Kyra miserable, not me. I need to speak to her again before next week.

"So, what trouble have you gotten yourself into today?"

My head snaps up, eyes fly open. I immediately find the source of the mocking voice: Mace.

"Are you following me?" I ask, ignoring his question.

"Well, I did ask you to read my note and meet me. If you'd done that, you wouldn't have walked past me this morning. So, yeah, I followed you. I was curious," he says, shrugging.

Well at least he's being honest this time.

"So what did you do?" he asks again, nodding at the house behind me.

"It doesn't matter what I did," I say. "It was a misunderstanding."

He smirks. "Fair enough. You want to hang out?"

"I can't," I say too quickly. "I mean, I would, maybe. But I have to be somewhere, and I haven't read your note yet. I'll read it tonight, okay?" I'm surprised at how confident I sound. There's no doubt that he makes me nervous, but in a good way.

"Well, you were supposed to do that last night, but okay, we can push it back a day. Not like we've got a limited amount of those. Oh, wait . . ."

"Ha-ha. I'll read it tonight."

"All right, all right. I'm only playing with you. So you really got to be somewhere?"

"Yep," I say. "Tomorrow, though?"

"Sure," he says, and winks.

My breath catches in my throat. All for such a small, insignificant gesture. I swallow and look back at him, even though my cheeks are flushed and I can feel them sizzling red-hot. Mace smiles at me. I study the dimple on his cheek and blush even more furiously.

I clear my throat. "Right, okay. Bye, then," I stutter.

I turn on my heel and march away, headed for home. It takes every effort not to look back, and I can feel his eyes on me.

Back home, I find Mom in her usual spot. She's asleep, though. Laying on the sofa with the Reports blaring out of the television set. I creep in and turn the volume down, careful not to wake her.

In the kitchen, I grab a glass and fill it with water, then make a sandwich and take it up to my room.

There's a quiet tap at my bedroom door. I don't need to open it to know who it is. Mom rarely comes up here to speak to me, especially not now. I cross the room and open the door quietly.

"Hi, Dad," I whisper.

"Hey, Sia. Want to sit in the kitchen or stay in your room?"

"Here's fine," I say. "I don't want to wake Mom."

He nods and takes a seat at my desk. I perch on the edge of my bed and wait.

"What is all of this about?" I ask.

Dad clears his throat. He runs his rough hands through his salt-and-pepper hair, then scratches his stubble, rubbing his jaw line over and over. The two of us sit awkwardly, the air thick with discomfort. "I feel a little lousy for not being around much over the past week or so. Things haven't been easy. I wanted to see how you were holding up. I'm thinking you know that we're not going to be chosen."

"Yeah, I realize that. I'm doing okay, I guess," I tell him.

"You don't have to be brave in front of me. I know this is horrible. I know you're probably bursting with questions, just like everybody else. Ask away, say what you think, you're only human."

"Human," I repeat, followed by a short laugh. "I don't think I know what human is anymore."

"What do you mean by that?"

"The people in charge are human, but what they're doing to us is barbaric. Killing people off who don't qualify for their New World. I've never heard of anything so awfully unfair."

Dad stands and comes to sit beside me on the bed. "I know, Sia. I know."

"I went to see Kyra today," I tell him. "I really thought they'd have been chosen as citizens of the New World, with Mr. Foxe being a doctor and all."

"He's a good doctor, too," Dad says.

"Exactly. And isn't that what they're looking for? It seems strange, doesn't it? How exactly do they decide who is good enough to live there, and who's unworthy and must stay and die. Who are they to decide? What makes them so special?"

"I'm afraid I don't know the answer to that," Dad says, stroking my hair.

"It doesn't matter, anyway. It's been decided. How we feel won't make any difference."

"I'm sorry, Sia."

"Don't be," I say, folding my arms and scowling so much that my face hurts.

"With all of this going on, I'm worried about the way the sector is heading," Dad continues.

"I've noticed," I say, pointing to my chin.

Dad lifts my head and sees the scab on my face for the first time. "What happened to you?"

"I had food and I was alone. Someone jumped me. It's fine, though."

"Don't brush it off. This is serious," Dad says. "It's getting dangerous out there. I want you to be careful. I don't want you going outside at all if you can help it, not on your own, and especially not at night."

Uh-oh, he's starting to sound like Mr. Foxe. Although I feel anything but safe, I'm not necessarily afraid of the people in the sector. They are the least of our worries. Still, I understand the seriousness of what my dad is asking of me.

"I get that, Dad," I tell him. "I really do. But I have to go out. I can't stay inside all the time. Especially with Mom the way she is. I don't want to be like her. I don't want to be like the Foxes."

"Sia—"

"No, Dad. I'll be careful, I promise. And I won't go out at night. But I'm not promising to stay in all day."

He sighs heavily. "I understand that it's a lot to ask. I'm just thinking of your safety. I suppose I can't force you. You wouldn't listen to me anyway, right?" He gives me a weak smile.

"I am listening to you. I said I'll stay in at night and be careful during the day. I just can't stay in *always*. It's not how I want to spend my time."

"How do you want to spend your time?"

It's a question I wasn't expecting. "I don't really know. I'm still trying to figure that out," I say, and leave it at that. I'm not willing to tell him about the list, or Mace.

Dad leans back so that his shoulders touch the wall. "Have you been watching the Reports at all?"

"No. Not really."

"Good," he says. "I don't want you to. They aren't doing anyone any good." I know he's thinking about Mom. "Have you spoken to your mother at all?"

"A little. Yesterday."

"Really? What did she say?"

"She just spoke about the walls and how we're trapped because of them. Not much more, really. She's terrified." I don't tell him about her lashing out and shouting at me. He doesn't need to know. It'll only upset him.

"Look after her, won't you?" he says.

His words anger me. "Why aren't you here looking after her?" I ask. "Maybe if you stayed home and spent

39

some time with us, or took us out of the house some-where, Mom might start to feel better."

Dad sits up. "It's not that simple. Please know that I am trying to help you and your mom. She won't go out. She won't even talk to me. She's glued to the Reports and won't turn them off. There's nothing else I can do other than what I am already doing."

"And what exactly is it you're doing?" I press.

He opens his mouth then closes it again. I wait. "I can't tell you," he finally says. "Not yet. Just know it's important and that I'm trying to help you. Please, don't worry."

I frown as he stands up to leave, ending on such a cryptic note. What the hell is he doing? He pats me on the top of my head, like he did when I was a little girl. I'm angry, so I move away from his hand. Hurt is clear on his face. I hope it's clear on mine, too.

"Be safe, Sia," he says as he leaves the room.

I run over to the door and lock it behind him. Leaning against it, I try to think of where he could possibly be going all the time, but come up with nothing. Why can't he tell me? Surely I can be trusted to keep it to myself for the next two weeks. Who could I tell, anyway? Mom?

My mind wanders back to Kyra. Dad seemed puzzled that the Foxes are still here, too. Nothing makes sense! I cross the room to my desk and pull out the notebook and pen. I add *Save Kyra* to the list. It looks selfish on paper, to drag her away from her family in the final days of her life. If they aren't going to the New World, Kyra should be able to choose how she lives the next fourteen days, shouldn't she?

I close the notebook and throw it into the drawer. There's no more stalling with Mace's note, so I take it out. A knot ties in my stomach, squeezing tight. I unfold the tattered paper.

Are you really okay with dying?

No, I think. I'm not okay with it. Of course I'm not. I read on:

Do you ever think that we could stand a chance?

No, I think again. This is something I've thought about over and over. I've thought of hiding, scaling the wall, smashing through it, everything. There's nothing we can do. We have no escape. We don't stand a chance.

I saw something in you. Something more than I see in most. At 9am, meet me where you fell the first time we met. I will explain more when I see you.

M

The knot tightens and I sit, stiff and uncomfortable, staring at the words on the page. I'm confused. I don't understand why he wants to meet me. What does he see in me that's so special and what does this mean for my last two weeks here?

I bite my lip, searching each possibility, and try to come to a decision. With not long to live, do I take the chance and meet him? Or do I stay away from the mysterious stranger who I only met a day ago? All I know is that I can't stop thinking about him.

I stare at the note some more, running my fingers over his handwriting.

I'm meeting him, I decide on impulse. If only to feed my curiosity.

Evening draws in quickly, and I hardly know where the day has gone before it's dark out and I am another few hours closer to my death.

I look out of my window, pressing my hand against the glass. The glow from the clock tints my skin red. Like blood. I stumble back and close the shutters.

I've been thinking about Kyra all day. I have to see her, now. But I promised Dad I'd stay in when it's dark out.

I pace my bedroom, biting my thumbnail. Dad's not home right now. If I'm really quick, he won't even know I left the house. And curfew is hours away.

Still dressed, I grab my backpack and head downstairs. I pull my boots on, then go into the kitchen before I leave. I slip a kitchen knife into my pack and head for the door.

I creep past the living room, the Reports still playing on low volume. I'm thankful for the slight sound that masks my opening and closing of the front door. Not that Mom would notice, anyway.

I run to Kyra's, fast. My lungs and throat burn as I pant for breath, but I keep going. It usually takes me around ten minutes to walk here, but I make it in five.

I throw tiny pieces of loose gravel at Kyra's window. The light is on, so I hope I catch her attention.

Around three throws later, the shutters open and Kyra peers out into the garden. Her face falls when she sees me. I wave and she opens the window.

"What are you doing?" she hisses.

"I came to help you," I say in a loud whisper back.

Her face screws up and her eyes narrow. "Help me what?"

"To get away from your family."

"I don't want to get away from my family!" she says, turning around like she's checking to see if anyone's behind her.

"Kyra, what's wrong with you? Earlier you were so miserable. I came to get you so that you can come and live with me. We can do all kinds of fun stuff before that day comes."

"That will never work. My parents will come looking for me and the first place they'll check is your house."

"Well, we can go somewhere else then—"

"You don't get it. I'm not coming with you. My family has actually got a chance of getting out of here. I can't jeopardize that by running away with you."

"Well, I—"

"No, Sia. Look, I'm glad that you're here, really. I wasn't happy about the way we left things and I hoped to get the chance to make it right. I don't think it's a good idea for us to see each other again. We should say goodbye now. You know that I love you, and I will keep you in my thoughts, but I just want to cut all ties now. You're the last one."

"No," I breathe. This isn't Kyra talking. This is her dad. It has to be. He's told her to say these things. "No," I repeat.

"Please don't make this harder. I'm sorry for the way things have turned out. I'm having a hard time coping and you caught me on a bad day. I love you, okay? I really do. Please know that. And please don't come back."

Kyra closes the window before I can say anything else. I find my voice again and I want to tell her that I love her, too. That I'm sorry, too. But she doesn't give me the chance. She's closed the window and the blackout shutters, locking me out of her life for good.

I blink back the tears that sting my eyes. *I won't cry*, I tell myself. *I can't cry.*

I run back home, the pain in my throat and chest matching the pain in my heart. I'll never see my best friend again.

I bound up the stairs once I get back to the house, not even trying to be quiet. I lock my bedroom door and throw myself into my desk chair, violently yanking open the drawer and flipping through the notebook with such force that I almost rip out each page I turn. How could Kyra treat me like that? Mr. Foxe must be making her push me away. He *must* be. She isn't like that; she wouldn't *do* that.

I just don't know what to think anymore.

I scribble harshly through my latest addition to the list involving Kyra. Little drops of water land in the ink on the page, making it run. I'm supposed to have one more day with her and now it's gone.

I remember all the time we spent together in my room after school, doing our homework or just talking until it got dark and Kyra's mom called to tell her to come home. We told each other secrets, shared problems we couldn't talk to anyone else about. I was always there for her when her dad was driving her nuts. And she always made me feel better the times Mom made me cry.

Sometimes we wouldn't go straight home from school; we'd just walk around the sector aimlessly like two fish in a tank. We had a few other friends, but not many. We were enough for each other. In a place where there is nothing to do, time seems to move so slowly, but with Kyra the hours would fly by. I'd give anything to have some of those hours back now.

I stop fighting and let myself cry.

13 DAYS

Today I'll see Mace.

I'm nervous, but also excited, despite everything that happened last night. I have no idea what he'll say to me, but I can't wait to find out. My stomach flips every time I think about it.

I have a couple hours until I meet him, so I decide to make pancakes for breakfast.

I run down the stairs in my pajamas. As I pass the living room, I poke my head inside to check on Mom. "Good morning," I say, but she is sleeping. The muted Reports are still on.

I turn to leave the room, but the images on the screen stop me. It's not the usual destroyed sectors airing.

It's the New World.

I don't want to see it. Inside, I'm screaming at myself to look away, but I can't. I've seen it before, but this time is different. The recording is showing people arriving in the city, ready to start their new lives.

Damien Hoist, the creator of the New World, waits to greet them and smiles for the cameras. I've seen this man's face once before, and I avoid seeing it again. He is responsible for all of this. I know there are others to blame now, too, but Damien Hoist started it. The very idea for the New World spilled from his lips.

The new citizens step out of the aircraft. It's a family of three—a mother, father, and a teenage girl.

Just like my family.

Except they can't be. They must have something special about them—something we lack—to be chosen when we are not. I wonder what they've done to earn their place.

I feel my mood start to sink as I drag myself away. In the kitchen, I collect the ingredients I need and attempt to block the New World from my mind as I dump them into a bowl. There is even a drop of syrup left in the bottom of the bottle. I turn it upside-down while I whisk the lumpy mixture.

The sweet, buttery smell of sizzling pancakes fills the entire kitchen and drifts through the house. I hear the front door open and close and my dad's footsteps coming along the hallway, pausing at the living room presumably to check on Mom as I did earlier. He enters the kitchen and inhales deeply.

"Mm," he says. "Looks like I came home at the right time."

I force a smile. "You sure did."

Dad looks at me for an extended moment, eyebrows raised. "Everything okay?"

"Fine," I say. "They're almost ready. Why don't you sit and I'll serve you?"

He does as I suggest, sitting on one of the rickety chairs around the kitchen table. I flip a pancake onto an empty plate and add syrup, then pour a glass of orange juice for him.

I set the plate and glass down in front of Dad.

"Thanks, Sia," he says with a grin on his face. He really does look happy right now.

"Eat up. I'll take the next plate to Mom."

I toss the freshly made pancake onto an empty plate and squeeze almost all of what's left from the bottle of syrup. I carry the plate and juice to the living room and set them down on the coffee table. I gently shake Mom to wake her. When she doesn't stir, I shake a little harder. Nothing.

"Mom?" I grip her shoulders, shaking her roughly now. She still doesn't wake up. I prop her into a sitting position and her head lolls back.

"Mom?" I say again, a sob escaping my lips.

I do the only thing I can think of and feel her neck for a pulse, which is something I learned in school. I can't find one, but I don't know if I'm doing it right. And my hands are shaking.

"Dad!" I shout, then look back at Mom. I thought the volume of my voice might've shocked her into wakefulness, but it didn't.

Oh, God. What's happening? I don't want to believe that she might be . . . dead. I move away suddenly, releasing her shoulders so she flops back onto the sofa like a ragdoll, landing at an awkward angle.

Dad enters the room, licking his fingers one by one. He looks at me, then at Mom. "What's the matter?" he says.

"She won't wake up."

He rushes over, checks her pulse, lifts her eyelids, places his ear next to her nose and mouth. "Oh, Sia," he breathes.

I know what he's going to say, and I know I don't want to hear those words. I look back at her.

And then I'm screaming.

Dad tries to take me back into the kitchen, but my feet are rooted to the spot and my screams are still pouring over my lips.

"Please, Sia. Please come and wait in the kitchen," he says, but I hardly hear him. "You don't need to see this."

I take a step in his direction. My movements feel mechanical as I force myself to keep going down the hallway and finally sit at the kitchen table. I think I've stopped screaming.

During the next hour, I don't move from my spot. I want to know what happened. I want to know *when* it happened. But I don't move, can't move. I just sit and listen, trying to remember to blink, to breathe.

Dad's been checking on me, but I haven't spoken to him yet. I've been listening to people coming and going from the house. The pancake mixture sits dripping on the countertop, the third plate and third glass waiting to be used.

I glance at the clock. 8:34 a.m. Half an hour until I see Mace. Except I'm not going anymore. How can I after what just happened? Mom's gone, and I don't know how or why. Am I to blame? Is Dad?

Finally, I drag myself off the wooden chair, pour a glass of water, and head to my bedroom. I don't want to cry or scream or shout. I don't want to *feel*.

I lie in bed. All I want is to fall asleep and escape this nightmare, though I imagine whatever is waiting for me in my dreams will be just as bad.

I remember my last conversation with Mom. Where she'd shouted at me and scratched my face. We hadn't spoken since. And now we never will. I touch my cheek, finding it wet. I didn't realize I was crying.

Through watery eyes, I look across the room at a photograph of Mom and me that I'd stuck in the edge of my mirror frame. Mom didn't like this photograph. She complained that slotting the picture in the side of my mirror for just about anyone to see was irresponsible. She didn't approve of individuality in a place where everything is the same.

I remember the night I moved my furniture around in my bedroom. I'd been over to my friends' houses and their rooms were *exactly* the same as mine. All but the photograph. So I swapped my bed with my desk, and my bookshelf with my mirror, and made it different. When I came home from school it'd all been moved back and Mom was sitting on my desk chair waiting for me. She yelled at me then. She told me never to do anything like that again, and that drawing attention to myself would get me into trouble.

I push the bedcovers back and approach the mirror on unsteady feet. Plucking the photograph out of the frame, I examine it closely. I'm looking back at myself, smiling brightly, but Mom's posture is awkward, her smile strained.

I look in the mirror and see my mom looking back at me now—not the girl in the photograph, not the girl I was, but a drained, pale face with sunken eyes rimmed with red, and dark tangled hair. My clothes hang looser on my body than they used to. I shake my head. Look again. This isn't me. I am nothing like her.

I take the photograph back to bed with me. Folding it in half, I tuck it under my pillow. It's the only one I have, but I don't want to look at it again.

I toss and turn, haunted by thoughts of Mom. It's a strange thing, death. Mom and I never really had a strong connection. We were never close or affectionate toward one another. Yet now that she's gone, I find myself spilling tears that I didn't know I held for her.

I remind myself that it was going to happen anyway, Mom's death. It just came early. I can't let this ruin me, *I can't*.

Thirteen days before I join her.

Thirteen days before the end.

Twelve will be a new day, a better day.

It has to be.

12 DAYS

It's not better.

I feel just as miserable this morning as I did yesterday. I sit up and remind myself that Mom was going to die anyway. We all are.

I get out of bed and unlock my door, feeling groggy after spending a whole day under the covers. I go look for Dad and find him asleep in his bed, a place I haven't seen him occupy for a week or more. I approach his side of the bed to wake him. As I shake him softly, I have visions of yesterday, of shaking Mom's dead body and trying to wake her. I feel sick and turn to leave, but Dad awakens and grabs my arm. I yelp and he releases me instantly.

"I'm sorry," he says.

It takes me a minute to catch my breath. "It's okay. I was just checking that you were all right."

"I've been so worried about you," he says.

I hang my head. "Sorry," I say, and I am.

Dad sits up and pats the mattress next to him for me to sit. But that's where Mom used to sleep before moving to the sofa. I shake my head. He seems to realize why and shuffles over to her side, freeing up his space. I sit and pull the covers over my legs. It's nice and warm where he's been sleeping.

We silently stay beside each other for a few moments. Neither of us know exactly how to start this conversation, to say something, anything, for the first time since the horrors of yesterday.

I spot Mom's slippers at the foot of the bed, her hairbrush on the nightstand beside an unfinished book. I speak first, just a whisper, though it shatters the silence. "How did it happen?"

Dad sighs, long and heavy. "Your mom, she—" His voice breaks. His eyes shine. He holds his tears, though. He won't let them fall, not when he's trying to be strong for me. I let out a smile, if only very slightly, at the similarities between us.

"Tell me," I say. "How did she do it?"

Silence follows my question for a long moment. Dad sighs again and closes his eyes. "It's unclear. She had more medication than she should have. She was dehydrated, starving, it's just . . . a whole mixture of things."

"Was it our fault?" I ask. "We neglected her, didn't we? We weren't there when she needed us most."

"No, Sia. No," Dad says. "You can't think like that. We *tried,* and our efforts proved useless. There is nothing that we could have done. There's nobody here that could have helped. It's those damn Reports. If you want to blame anything, blame them. They're . . . they're evil."

"Evil?"

"Your mom isn't the only person in this sector to be sucked in to watching them all day, every day. She isn't the first to take her own life, either. Many have done the same, driven by fear after seeing what is aired on those Reports. It's too much to watch and wait for it to happen to you."

I ball my hands into fists by my sides, so angry with the people that are doing this to us. Frightening us until they kill us, or until we kill ourselves.

"We've got each other," Dad says. "It's just you and me now, and we'll be okay. I promise."

It's a promise I know he can't keep. We won't be okay. We both know that.

He leans over to wrap his arm around me. "What time is it?"

"It's six-thirty."

"And the day? I've lost track."

"We have twelve days left," I reply with certainty. I never forget, never lose track of when my life will end.

"Right," he says, strained. "Not long, then."

"No, it's not."

Dad takes his arm back from around my shoulder and rubs his face with both hands. "I better get going. I missed a lot yesterday," he says, still giving nothing away about where he's going or what he's missed. "Will you be okay here alone? I can stay if you need me." He's already gathering his clothes, though, and heading to his bathroom.

I push the covers back and flip my legs over the side of the bed. "No, of course. It's fine," I say. "You go. I've got things to do anyway."

He shoots an uncertain glance my way. "Be careful, okay? Remember what I said about it not being safe out there."

"I remember, Dad. Don't worry."

Determined to get back to normal, or as normal as things can be, I take a long shower, washing my hair with a fruity shampoo that's running low. Thoughts of Mom dying alone force themselves back into my mind, though. I can't fully get my head around it. She's gone. It just doesn't feel real.

She was gone way before now, I tell myself. The mom I knew already died; I already grieved for her. A quiet, peaceful death is all she wanted. The rest of us face unimaginable horror—blood, suffering, destruction.

I shake my head in an attempt to banish dark thoughts. *Remember the list,* I remind myself. *Remember your life is almost over. Don't waste it.*

I put on a bit of make-up after I towel off—mascara, blush, and lip balm, which softens my lips. I usually tie my hair back into a high, messy bun on top of my head. Today, I experiment wearing it down, but in the end drag it back up and wear it the way I always do. I'm more comfortable this way. While I dress, a bit of the excitement I felt yesterday morning races back as I get ready to find Mace. I'm not sure where he'll be, but I feel compelled, somehow, to meet him, despite what happened yesterday. I have to find out what he wants from me—I can't stop thinking about his note.

Before leaving the house, I call the Foxes'. No one answers. I leave a message, telling Kyra what happened to my mom. It's a short message, and I struggle to keep my voice steady.

I set out at 9:00 a.m. to find Mace. I head to the meeting place in his letter, but stop by the food store on the way in case he's working. I enter cautiously, unsure of what I might find inside. It was bad enough three days ago, and as expected, it's a total disaster zone now. There is near to nothing left on the shelves. Everything has either been taken or ruined. It smells sour and bitter with all the spoiled food. I pull my T-shirt over my face, to cover my nose and mouth, and edge in a little more.

"Mace!" I yell. "Mace, are you here? It's Sia!"

I hear rustling and clanging of tins as they hit the tiled floor. I stand still, hardly daring to breathe. I let the shirt fall from my face and take a step back. "M-Mace?" I say more quietly. "Is that you?"

Three figures emerge from an aisle. I can only see their shapes in the poor light. I feel as though I'm in a zombie movie, the way their backs are arched and their walk is slow and menacing.

"Who ...Who are you?" I stutter. They continue moving toward me without answering.

Once they step into the light I can see them more clearly. Two adult men and a woman, their hands and mouths dirty with the food they've been scraping from tins. They look as if they haven't washed in days. Their hair is thick with grease and their skin is covered with grime.

They remind me of my mom, but worse. Is this how she'd have turned out if she hadn't died?

I shudder and push the thought aside.

I back up toward the exit, too scared to run. Dad told me it was getting worse; I just didn't realize how much worse. The three stop approaching me and watch as I exit the store.

As soon as I step outside, I turn and run.

I'm still running when I see Mace in the distance, standing, waiting.

"Mace!" I scream. My throat is sore, my voice raspy and cracked, my breathing painful and rapid. His head jerks up. He starts moving toward me.

I stumble a little, my legs giving way beneath me due to fear and exhaustion. I keep running, though, until I reach him. He clutches both my arms with his warm hands to stop me from falling. My legs shake and I can't catch my breath.

"Sia, are you okay?" he asks. He scans the empty street. "Is someone chasing you?"

"No. Food . . . store . . . crazy," I heave. I can't speak. I can't stop trembling. My heart is racing, crashing against my ribs. My hands are shaking.

"Sia," Mace says, crouching down and looking into my eyes. "You're scaring me."

I close my eyes and shake my head. It's all I can do. I've never run so fast, so far, in my life.

"Come on," Mace says. "We shouldn't stay here."

We start walking and I stumble a little, my calf muscles cramping. Mace scoops one strong arm under my legs and wraps his other behind my back. He lifts me and holds me close to his chest. My heart rate increases.

At first it feels strange to be so near to someone I hardly know, but as his grip tightens and he walks us away from danger, I start to relax into him a little. I close my eyes and rest my head on his shoulder, enjoying his warmth. Inhaling his crisp, earthy scent calms me, and my breathing slows, my heartbeat falls back to a steady rhythm, and my hands stop trembling.

Just as I was beginning to completely relax in his arms he stops and sits me gently down on the ground. I feel grassy earth beneath me but I haven't yet opened my eyes. When I do, I see that we're beside the lake. It's calm. There's no one around and there are no cameras here by the lake or up on the hill.

Mace kneels in front of me, placing his hand on my forehead, checking my temperature. "How're you feeling?" he says.

"I'm okay," I respond. He runs his hand down my cheek to my jaw, before letting go. "I went to the store to look for you. There were these people there . . ."

"It's all right, you're safe now," he says, touching my hand. My skin sparks as his fingers brush mine. I try to ignore the feeling as he circles his thumb over my hand.

"Who are they? What are they doing there?" I finally manage to ask.

Mace settles his thumb, but doesn't let go of my hand. "They're the people that were too late when everyone pan- icked and stocked up on food. Almost everything was gone by the time they got to the store. So they just stay there and pick at whatever's left. Anyone who enters the store they perceive as invading territory that they've claimed. Why were you there, anyway? I told you where I'd be in the note."

"I didn't come yesterday like you asked. I . . . I had other things to deal with. So I came looking for you today and stopped there on my way. It's where you were when we met. I wasn't sure if you'd still be waiting for me after I'd let you down twice."

"I wasn't waiting there the whole time, Sia." His shoulders shake with soft laughter. "I have been going back every morning, though. Just in case you decided to show."

"Oh," I breathe. "I guess I thought you'd have given up on me by now."

He watches me closely and my stomach flips. "I'm just glad you finally came," he says. "Even if it was only by chance that you saw me when you were running for your life."

I smile. He hadn't given up on me. He kept going back there because he wanted me to come. My smile widens. I start to wonder when he's going to talk to me about what it is he "saw in me." Should I bring it up first?

"What are you thinking about?" Mace asks.

"Your note," I say.

"Ah, you read it. And?"

I shrug. "I have some questions."

"And I will answer them. First, I'm thinking about what we can do today. Any thoughts?"

I look at the lake, thinking about my list. But I'm not ready. I can't swim and have nothing to keep me afloat. Then my gaze travels up the hill. I point at it. "A race to the top?"

Mace turns, squinting against the early sun. "Seriously?"

"Yes! Have you ever been up there?" I ask.

"No, it's forbidden," he says, but I don't see him as the type to follow the rules. "Why do you want to go up there anyway?"

"I just want to see something more than this sector before I die. Our only view is that ugly metal wall that matches the same miserable gray color as everything else. I want to see what's out there."

"Wow. Not a fan of the sector, I see."

I smile. "Nope. It's boring."

"I can't disagree," he says, jumping to his feet and holding out his hand to help me up. "Let's go. But if we're caught, it's on you." He smirks.

"Fine," I grumble playfully.

The grass on the hill has grown long and thick and my feet keep getting stuck in tangles of weeds. I trip and reach out to break my fall. Mace's arms wrap around my waist before I hit the ground and he balances me. We decide to abandon the race idea.

We come to a chain link fence about halfway up that stops us. The top of the fence is lined with barbed wire, so we can't climb over. Mace kicks it.

"There must be a way through," he says.

"Maybe we should turn back," I say glumly.

Mace feels along the fence and I follow. Just when I start thinking all of this has been a huge waste of time, his arm goes through a broken section.

"Here!"

He widens the gap for me so I can crawl through, then he follows. I laugh and he smiles back at me, and we continue up to the top.

My hands and knees are covered in dry mud by the time we make it.

I close my eyes for a moment, readying myself for what I'm about to see. Now that I'm here I'm almost afraid to look out. But, slowly, I open my eyes and take in the land beyond the sector. Mace stands beside me, equally quiet.

"Wow," I breathe.

"I know."

There are no people, no buildings, no *gray*. The land is made up of only lush, green grass and red, yellow, and white flowers.

"I've never seen a real flower before," I say.

"Neither have I," Mace replies, and I realize how sad that is. A beautiful land with so much color and texture lies beyond our metal walls and we'll never get to feel those same flowers with our own hands. At least now I've seen them with my own eyes.

There are trees out there, too. Huge, towering trees with thick trunks and full branches covered in thousands of leaves. The branches sway gently in the soft breeze. It's hypnotizing.

We stay on the hill for hours, enjoying the fresh air and staring at the beautiful landscape. Finally, I can tick something off my to-do list, instead of crossing things off that will never be completed.

At first I was paranoid that someone might catch us up here, but as time goes by I start to feel like nothing else exists. I feel so relaxed up here, at peace. It makes me wonder what death will be like. After all the chaos and horror that'll take place in the sector, will we get this when it's all over?

I glance at Mace. He's lying on his back with one tattoo-covered arm propping his head up. His eyes are closed. I watch the wind whipping his dark hair around his face. His eyelids flicker, his lashes brush against his skin. The sun shines on his face, soft and golden. For a minute I forget all that is happening down in the sector and soak up everything about this stolen moment that's just for us.

"I can see you looking, you know?" he says.

I jump. "I was wondering if you were awake, that's all."

"Yeah, yeah," he mocks. "Well, I am awake. I was awake the whole time you were staring at me."

My cheeks burn. I know they're bright red, especially with the blush I added this morning, but I can't stop them flaring up. I try for a change of subject, eager for answers about his note. "So, why did you want to meet me?"

Mace sits up. His face shifts from playful to serious. "Do you remember when we met and you saw my name badge and ran away? Well, I don't work at the food store. Never have."

"What were you doing there?"

"Scouting. I'm stationed at the store. Or, I was. I was there to recruit." I watch him, puzzled. "We're fighting back, Sia," he adds.

"Who is 'we'?" I ask. I keep my voice steady, my eyes fixed on his, even though it's difficult to mask the disappointment I feel inside. I thought he *liked* me. I thought he'd asked me to meet him because he liked me and wanted to get to know me. But now it seems as though I'm only here because he wants me to fight with some group he's involved in.

"Well, so far there's around twenty of us. We're adding new members every day, but we have to be careful about it. They're still watching us on the cameras. That's why we've stopped hitting the same places to recruit."

"So, that's it? Twenty of you? Do you think that's enough to fight back with?"

"We're getting good and training every day."

"Mace, they're *machines*. You're training to fight machines. No one has survived an attack yet, and I'm sure many have tried to fight back."

"Whoa," he says, scowling and looking away from me. "Thanks for your support."

I sigh and sit up straighter. "I'm being realistic."

"So, you've just given up? You're not even going to try? When they come, you'll just stand there and let them kill you?"

"I don't see it any other way! I've accepted that I'm going to die. Maybe you should, too."

Upset and angry, I stand and begin walking away without giving him a chance to respond. I pick up my pace going down the steep hill, stumbling between the bushes with no one to help me back up when I tumble. Just a few hours in his company and I'd managed to forget about all the horrible things that have happened and will happen. I fooled myself into thinking it was because of *him*. We both climbed this hill for very different reasons today. I never should have come in the first place, but I felt so alone this morning and was excited to have someone new in my life after losing so many so quickly.

I hear him following me, but I'm determined not to let him catch up. I don't want to hear anything else he has to say. But he's getting closer and I know I can't outrun him. Even if I make it to the bottom of the hill, I'll still have to get around the lake and through the streets before I reach home.

I crouch down to obscure my movements and run a little farther downhill. I'm sure he hears me stumbling and crashing through overgrown bushes. They rustle and give my position away.

I find a place to hide, rolling under a thick bush. I try to stop panting. Bushes don't pant. And if Mace walks by one that does, it'll be a dead giveaway that I'm under it.

I hear rustling and hold my breath, even though it pains me to do so when I need oxygen so desperately. The noise fades as Mace passes by. I exhale, relieved. Part of me knows how pathetic I'm being, running away from him like that. But I was afraid of what I might have said if I'd stayed with him. I'm not sure I could have held myself together or kept my disappointment in our meeting hidden.

My chest continues to heave and ache. I can't get enough air, and I can't muster the energy to move from under the cover of the leaves. I lie flat on my back and prop my knees up instead, waiting to regain some strength.

The sound of someone close by startles me.

A hand reaches under the bush and grabs my arm, yanking me hard. I stop the scream that's working its way up my throat. Whoever it is pulls at me with plenty of effort, but I don't budge.

The leaves part and I see wide blue eyes staring at me. It's a girl. The gap widens between the branches, and she climbs under the leaves, sitting across from me with her knees pulled to her chest. In the small cramped space, I see every detail of her—every blonde strand of knotted hair, every speck of dirt on her face, and every tear track through that dirt.

"Who are we hiding from?" she says in a soft voice.

I shake my head. "It doesn't matter. I think he's gone."

"Oh, so it's a he? I saw a boy go by. He was heading back down to the sector." She shakes her head. "I don't know why anyone would go back down there. Are you staying here?"

"What? No. I'm going back, too."

She stares at me for a few uncomfortable moments, then shrugs. "Can we get out from under here now? Is it safe?"

I study her curiously. "I guess." We shuffle out in turn. I straighten up and brush the dirt and leaves from my hair. "Who are you?" I ask.

"Lilly," she says.

"I'm Sia."

"I know who you are. I heard *him* calling your name." She reaches hold of my arm and starts walking uphill again, taking me with her.

"Where are we going?"

"Home," Lilly says.

"I already told you I'm not staying. My home is down there. Isn't yours?"

"No," Lilly says. "I live here."

I gasp and stop walking. "Are you from the Rough?"

Lilly laughs. "No. Even if I was, how would I have gotten in here?"

"I don't know. There could be a secret passage or something."

"Well there's not, and I'm not from the Rough. I used to live in one of the houses in the sector, but now I live up here." She gives my arm a tug. "Will you visit? Just for a little while."

I yank my arm from her grasp a little more roughly than I mean to. "I—"

"Please. I haven't seen anyone for a week and I'm frightened," she says.

Lilly looks around my age, possibly younger, and seems fairly harmless. "Okay," I say hesitantly. "But only for a little while, then I have to get back." She beams at me and starts walking uphill again. I follow.

Before long, we stop at a small clearing. There's a backpack and a sleeping bag bunched together on the ground. There's a lot of litter scattered around, too. It looks like she's tried to keep it under control, but the bags she's been using for trash are full and their contents are spilling over. I hate seeing litter on the ground. This place is ugly enough without adding to it with trash. But what does it matter now? The sector will be destroyed and littered with bodies soon—what do a couple of food wrappers matter against that?

Using a box of matches, Lilly lights a disposable barbeque. There's a whole pile of them stacked up to the side. Some used, some unused. Once lit, we settle down around the fire.

"How did you get through the fence?" I ask. She lifts up a pair or pliers and snips them together in answer. "And you brought all of this stuff up here by yourself, without anyone seeing you?"

"Finn helped me," she says, and the name sounds familiar. "He's my next-door neighbor. Well, he was. He's the only person who knows where I am. How many days are left?"

"Twelve," I say on autopilot.

"Feels like I've been here longer."

I stare at her, puzzled. "Why aren't you at home?"

"I can't go home." She holds her hands out in front of the flames.

"But, what about your parents? Won't they be worried?"

"I doubt that," she says. "They're in the New World." I inhale loudly and Lilly smirks. "Well, I expect they are by now, anyway," she adds.

"You were chosen? *Why are you still here?*"

"Yeah, we were chosen," she says, like it's nothing. I find that I'm angry all of a sudden. It means a lot to be chosen. It means you're worth something. Lilly doesn't seem to appreciate it as much as she should. "My mom and dad are musicians. They're really talented. My two younger sisters play, too."

"And you don't? Is that why you had to stay?"

"No. I play. I'm still here because I chose not to go with them. I don't want to go there and be a part of that. My family were thankful to have been spared the fate the rest of the sector's citizens share. They replied instantly, agreeing to go. They didn't even think twice about it."

"Well, why would you?" I ask. Lilly's making no sense. I'd leave here in a heartbeat.

"Because it's an evil place, run by evil people," she spits and I startle at the sudden change in her tone. "As soon as they accepted the invite, my parents packed up my younger sisters' belongings and then started on their own. I stayed in my room, thinking about it and looking through the electronic leaflet the New World sent us. Then I told them I didn't want to go."

"What did they say?"

"Nothing that I wanted to hear. I told them that I don't agree with what the New World is doing. I begged them not to go there. Begged them so hard not to go to that place."

"But they still did."

Lilly nods. "Yes. They told me to gather my things. So I did. But instead of going with them, I went to Finn, and then here," she says, sweeping her arm to the side. "My parents agreed with my reasons, but they wouldn't stay, not even for me. Going there was their only chance to save my two little sisters. So they went, and I stayed. Now my sisters will grow up in that wretched world— in a family of four instead of five—" Lilly's voice breaks for a moment. "I was terrified of staying, and terrified of leaving. In the end, I couldn't face going to that place and being one of them. I couldn't have lived happily ever after in the New World while the people left behind in the sector suffer."

"Staying here means you'll die, though."

"No it doesn't," she says shortly. "I'm hidden. They won't find me up here."

"Lilly, no one has stayed hidden in the other sectors. Everyone was found. There have been no survivors. You should go if you still have the chance."

"Leaving isn't an option for me, Sia. I can't do it. And how do you know there were no survivors? They aren't likely to jump out in front of the cameras and boast about it. I'll be all right up here. Why would they send the machines up this hill?"

"They'll send them everywhere," I say.

"You're *just* like my family. They didn't listen to me, either."

"I am listening—"

"I haven't given up all hope of staying alive. This *will* work, I'm telling you. There are no cameras up here. No one knows I'm here."

My thoughts sidetrack to Mace, another person doing what he can to try to stay alive. What's wrong with me? While they're both trying to save their lives, I'm just accepting that mine is already lost. How does that make me any different from my mom?

I want to tell Lilly about Mace and his group, but I don't. She seems set on hiding and hoping the machines don't find her. There is one small thing I can do to help her, though. And it's something that'll benefit both of us. "Do you need anything, Lilly?" I ask. "I can come visit you sometimes and bring you some food."

She looks delighted. "I'd like that a lot," she says and I smile, happy to be given a purpose, to have something to do, someone to talk to, someone to distract me for the next twelve days.

It's beginning to go dark when I part with Lilly. She walks partway down the hill with me but won't come any closer to the sector than the fence.

I walk quickly, checking the shadows. It's horribly quiet. For once, I actually hope my dad isn't home because he'll be furious with me for staying out so late.

I jog up the path leading to my front door and fumble with my key. There's movement in the shadows and I gasp, dropping my keys. Then a dark figure steps out from beside the neighboring house. I don't know whether to run or grab the keys and try to get the door unlocked and open. I don't think I have a chance either way, so I bang my fists on the door and shout for my dad. He doesn't answer.

The figure steps out of the shadows. "No one's home."

"Mace?" I say. "What are you doing here? You scared me!"

I bend down to pick up my keys, and when I stand up again, his face is right in front of mine. So close, we're almost touching. I feel his breath on my face, warm and sweet.

"I looked everywhere for you, Sia. Why'd you run away? I'm sorry if you thought I was using you in any way to get you to be part of this group. I thought you'd want to help us fight."

"Well, you were wrong," I say stubbornly.

"Obviously. Anyway, I just wanted to make sure you were all right."

He shoves his hands in his pockets and turns away from me, making his way down the path.

He stops suddenly and looks over his shoulder. "See you around," he says, and half-raises a hand to wave goodbye.

No, don't go, I think but don't say it. I watch him walk away instead.

I unlock the front door and flip the light-switch. The door to the living room is open. I step inside. It's dark, cold, empty. I linger for a moment, looking at the blank TV screen that'd been constantly turned on before.

I sit on the coffee table and pick up the TV remote, turning it over in my hand. The numbers on the buttons are scratched away, some are even missing where Mom picked them out and dropped them on the floor. I throw it back on the sofa and stand up. I can't bear to be in here. It's too soon.

I leave the hall light on for when, or if, Dad comes home, and head up to my room. I'm hungry but fatigue wins out. It's been a long day and all I want is my pajamas, my bed, and sleep.

I crawl into bed and turn out the lights, but my eyes won't close. My stomach growls, keeping me up. I lie awake. I feel sad and can't shake it off. Is the sadness for Mom? Or Dad, Kyra, or Lilly? Or is it because of the way I left things with Mace? I should have called him back when I had the chance.

I switch the light back on and head to my desk, pulling the drawer open and grabbing my notebook as I sit down. I flick through it to my list, thinking it'll make me feel better to check something off. I'd climbed the sector's hill, and seeing out beyond the walls was incredible. But why don't I feel incredible?

I make a check mark next to it, but it doesn't make me feel better. It just makes me think about how I ruined what could have been an almost perfect day.

I look at the list and realize how pathetic it really is. The few things left make me think of how I won't be able do all the things I should be able to do in life. I'll never grow up. I'm limited to only these trite things because my life is going to be cut short—because I know when it'll end, because it's getting closer to that day.

I rip out the page, screw it into a ball, and throw the list away. It was a dumb thing to write, anyway. I was stupid to think I could control the last days of my life with just a list.

I'd been handed a few choices today: accept my death, hide, or stand up and fight. Have I made the wrong one in accepting the way things are and giving up? Because that's what I'm doing, that's what it boils down to—giving up. I don't have false hope, like Mace. I don't want to hide, like Lilly. I want to cherish my last days; I want to enjoy them. Instead, I'm doing everything but.

This isn't how things are supposed to be.

I'm afraid of failing. I'm afraid of wanting to live, to fight, and not succeeding. But what's the alternative? Waiting to die? Should I let them kill me when they come or should I die fighting for my life? Because I still don't think any of us left behind stand a chance.

I eat an old, mushed-up oat bar sitting on my desk and go back to bed, abandoning my thoughts. I turn out the light. Tomorrow I'll set things right with Mace. I don't know what I'll say, and I haven't completely made up my mind about him yet, but it can't hurt to find out more about this group if I'm even going to consider putting up a fight. I close my eyes and drift off easily now that I've taken the edge off my hunger and hashed out my thoughts.

Another day gone.

11 DAYS

I'm lost.

And I have eleven days to find myself.

I'm eager to go looking for Mace from the moment I wake, but I doubt I'll run into him this early. Curfew has only just been lifted. The shutters have only just been unlocked.

I make some breakfast and decide to take leftovers up the hill to Lilly, then to look for Mace in the afternoon. I make oatmeal and wrap Lilly's bowl in foil, then eat mine at the kitchen table, listening to the *drip, drip, drip* of the tap water, and the *tick, tick, tick* of the clock, reminding me of what little time I have left. Once I'm done, I put Lilly's bowl in my backpack and head out the door.

As I trudge up the hill for the second day in a row, I'm careful not to swish the contents of my bag around too much so that the oatmeal won't seep out from under the foil and coat everything in sticky goo.

Lilly finds me before I find her.

"Hi," she says. "You came back."

"I promised, didn't I?" Lilly plays with a strand of knotted hair, twirling it around her finger. "I've brought you some breakfast, too," I say.

She smiles and takes my hand. "Come on."

We head the rest of the way up the hill together. My anticipation to reach the top grows as we climb higher and higher. I can't wait to see outside the walls again.

Once we find a clearing, Lilly sits on the grass without even glancing at the view in front of us. I take a moment before joining her.

"Isn't it brilliant?" I say. "All that open land, all those trees and flowers."

"Mm."

I look back at her. Her head is down, and she's pulling at the blades of grass by her feet.

"What is it?" I ask.

"I don't like looking at it," she says.

"Why? It's amazing!"

"Yeah. It is. But we'll never be able to get to it. We'll never climb those trees or pick those flowers. We can see it, but we'll never be able to reach it. So what's the point in looking at it and wanting it?"

"I never thought of it like that," I mumble and sit by her feet, facing her. I pick at the grass, too, to occupy my hands.

"I can't believe this is happening," Lilly sighs. "It makes you feel so small and insignificant, doesn't it—the way our lives can be snuffed out so easily? We're like ants burning under a magnifying glass. Hopeless, helpless. And there's not a thing we can do to stop it."

I shiver, even though the breeze isn't strong at all. "Can we talk about something else?"

Lilly shrugs. "You should just stay up here with me until it's over, you know. I wouldn't mind sharing. The company would be nice."

I shake my head. "I'm sorry, I can't."

She frowns. "Well, where *do* you live?"

"Second Street. On the far side of town."

"Oh, that's not far from me. I'm on Fourth—*was* on Fourth."

"I have a friend on Fourth. I thought her family would be chosen for the New World. But they haven't gone yet, and now I'm not sure they will. When did you get your invitation?"

"About two weeks ago. But I guess there's still time."

My stomach drops. *Two weeks.* "I hope so."

I look back to the Rough. It's not cloudy today, so the sunrays bounce off the ground, creating colors more vivid and spectacular than I saw yesterday. I watch the birds fly over us, going wherever they desire. I wish they'd come here sometimes and sing outside my window in the mornings. I listen to them now, but I can hear something else, too. It's quiet, distant—low and grumbling.

"Do you hear that?" I say. The sound grows and grows until it cancels out the birds completely. They burst from the trees and fly away. I wish I could do the same.

Lilly gasps and springs to her feet. "Hide!" She clamps down on my wrist, wrapping her fingers around it with a vice-like grip, and drags me down the hill.

"What is it?" I say, panting.

"It's one of the New World aircrafts. We can't let them see us up here."

I pull my arm from her grasp. "An aircraft? Coming here? It's the middle of the day." I turn my gaze back to the sky. "It might be—"

"Yeah. You might find out if your friend is going after all."

"I have to go," I say, turning around.

She grabs my shoulder. "*Don't* let them see you."

With no time for goodbyes, we run in opposite directions. Lilly heads for the thick bushes to hide. I crouch low and run as fast as I can down the hill, trying not to trip on snaking vines and twisting weeds. I head back to the familiar flat roads of the sector to see who'll be taken this time.

I regularly check the sky as I run. I can make out the black bulk of metal in the distance, gliding through the air. I'm swallowed by its shadow when it passes overhead. I can smell the fumes and the low grumble becomes a loud growl. I follow its course as it dips lower to the ground.

It's landing a few streets from my own. My heart leaps. *Kyra?*

But as I get closer I see it's too far out to be for her family. I curse with disappointment.

When I reach the street where the aircraft is landing, the force of the wind is brutal. I cover my eyes and move forward into the crowd that's already gathered to see who has been chosen.

The New Worlders are heavily armed. Four of them emerge from the aircraft outside the home of the chosen family. Two approach the house while the other two control the crowd. None of the citizens seem to notice the guns that are trained on them. I do. And I tell myself to leave, but I'm too desperate to see who comes out of that house to walk away now. I squeeze myself into a good spot and wait for the door to open.

The two New Worlders knock, and the front door swings inward. A tall, skinny man fills the doorway and I recognize him instantly as one of the teachers at the high school. Mr. Elvin. His wife also teaches there, but I never had any classes with her.

I know they have three young children, the eldest being eight, and I find that I'm happy for them. I don't want anyone to suffer here on Day Zero, especially not children.

Mr. Elvin narrows his eyes behind his thick-rimmed glasses and glares at the gathering, clearly not happy to have an audience. He ushers his sons out of the door and hands them over to the two New Worlders, who walk them to the aircraft.

The eldest seems to take after his father. He's tall with an air of intelligence, and he's clearly a leader—he takes the hands of his two younger twin siblings in a protective way. The twins walk on either side of their brother, holding on tightly. They have stuffed animals in their free hands. The toys' tails drag along the ground, gathering dirt. The twins are crying.

Once they're safe inside the aircraft, Mr. and Mrs. Elvin gather the rest of their belongings and exit their home for the last time. The two of them walk quickly, staring ahead, not making eye contact with anyone.

Mrs. Elvin is shaking. From what I know of her, she's shy and quiet. Her students could get away with just about anything in her class. She keeps her eyes trained on the aircraft like nothing else exists. *Just a little farther*, I think. *Then you'll be safe.*

Loud voices rise from the thick of the murmuring crowd. Mrs. Elvin's eyes bulge and she and her husband break out into a run.

People are yelling now, aggressive, hostile. My view is blocked when the crowd around me starts moving. Using the wall to steady myself, I climb onto a metal trashcan standing at the side of someone's house to get a better look. Now I can see over every head.

The aircraft is rocking. Bodies are crawling all over it and hanging off the sides. The crowd went from curious to chaotic in seconds. Some are trying to break inside. Some are trying to damage the aircraft. Some are banging on the windows in an attempt to break them. Mr. and Mrs. Elvin have been pushed back. Their boys are inside the craft, but the Elvins can't get close enough to protect them from their own neighbors.

Rebellion.

I should leave before the New Worlders start using their guns.

As I try to get down from my perch, the crowd surges forward, knocking me to the ground. I fall in a heap, and the contents of the trashcan topple out over my shoes. I get to my feet before I am trampled, putting my hand in something sticky.

As I try to get away from the aircraft, I'm shoved from side to side and lose sight of what's happening and of which way I should be moving. It's like battling against the violent waves of a stormy, unforgiving ocean. Every time I move forward I get knocked right back again. I'm encased in a shell of bodies and I can't break through the gaps. I start to panic as the crowd rushes, terrified of going under.

I'm pushed endlessly. I don't think it'll ever stop. I wind up back against the wall where I started. People are crashing into me, crushing me harder against the wall to the point where it becomes difficult to breathe. I call out to them, but it's no use. They don't even notice me.

Then I hear my name.

But is it my name? I can't be sure. There's so much noise around me it's hard to tell.

I see a figure, forcing its way through the swarm of bodies. It's Mace. He's here.

Mace heads toward me, but the crowd is so tightly packed that his approach is slowed. I don't know how much longer I can stay on my feet. Someone slams into me and I lose sight of Mace. I'm knocked hard against the wall. An elbow connects with my windpipe. I gasp, which hurts. I hold my hand to my throat and sink to the ground in agony.

It's dark down here, and legs kick at me from either side. Tears spill from my eyes. A hand reaches through the packed bodies and grabs my arm, pulling me up. I scream as my hands are torn from around my neck, but the sound comes out scratchy and rough and only brings more pain.

Mace throws me over his shoulder. No time to be gentle. He holds my legs strongly against his chest. I don't like it. I feel vulnerable.

81

I feel him pushing his way out of the crowd to where the street is less crammed, and then he keeps moving.

Gun shots.

I cover my ears and squeeze my eyes shut. More follow, and Mace is now jogging.

Before long we stop outside my house and Mace knocks on the door. He lowers me to my feet and I straighten out my shirt, which has ridden up my back.

"Thank you," I whisper, because that's all I can do.

He runs his hand down my neck and I flinch. "You're hurt," he says.

I nod and pull away to feel around in my backpack for my keys. "Nobody is home," I croak.

"Should I come inside with you? To make sure you're okay?"

"I think I'll be fine," I whisper, then regret it. Why didn't I say yes?

"Only if you're sure. I don't want to leave if you're not all right."

"I'll be fine," I say. "Really."

Dad could come home at any time and I've forgotten everything I wanted to say to Mace. I don't feel like I could even get the words out if I remembered them. My throat is throbbing and stings each time I swallow. My eyes are brimming with tears that I'm trying to hold back.

"I'll come by tomorrow and check on you, all right?"

I nod. "Thanks. For helping me, I mean. I don't know what would have happened to me if you hadn't been there."

Mace gathers me into his arms and touches his lips to my temple. "I'll see you tomorrow," he whispers into my ear.

I sit on the bottom step of the staircase and run my fingers through my hair, balling my hands into fists and pulling at the roots.

My mind whirls. I don't know what I want anymore. I don't think I even knew to start with, not really. I can't cope with it any longer—the confusion, the restlessness, the indecision.

What is *wrong* with me? I'm furious at myself. I felt so helpless back out in the street. What would have happened if Mace hadn't been there? Even if I don't make it past Day Zero, I need to be able to survive until then. If I want to make the most of my final days, I should know how to protect myself.

If I join Mace's group, I can learn that.

I'm so afraid, though. So scared to get close to Mace. I don't want to grow too attached to him, to want him too badly. I thought I did, but now it's happening and I'm caring for him, it terrifies me.

Why did I want to meet a boy and fall in love? Why make the end of my life harder on myself? It was different when it was just words on paper, when I didn't know who he was, when I didn't know how I'd really feel.

I imagine the machines coming here. I imagine them ripping Mace in half right before my eyes. I imagine his blood drenching his torn clothing. I imagine my screams as it's the last thing I see before the same happens to me. How can I fall for him knowing that that is our future?

Dad comes through the door and my eyes fly open. I let go of my hair, my hands dropping heavily to my sides. My whole body slumps. Dad studies me for a moment.

"Why are you sitting in the dark?" he asks, closing the door behind him and flicking the hallway light on. "Sia," he gasps when he gets a good look at me. "What happened to you?"

I sigh, and it hurts. "There was a riot in the sector. An aircraft came to collect a new family and people started going crazy and attacking the New Worlders," I tell him. I don't even know how it ended. I don't know if the boys were okay or if their parents ever made it to the craft.

"You were there?" he says, eyes widening. "I told you that it's dangerous in the sector. You promised me you'd be careful."

"I didn't know something like that would happen! I thought the aircrafts only came after curfew. Why was it even here in the middle of the day?" I clutch at my throat, the pain from speaking almost unbearable.

"Let me see your neck."

"I'll be all right."

"Tell me what hurts."

My entire body. "Just my throat. I'll be okay."

"I hate the thought of someone hurting you," Dad says, touching my shoulder.

"We've got a lot worse coming, Dad," I say with a short laugh, which turns into a ragged cough. He brings me a glass of water from the kitchen and I take it upstairs.

Hot water rushes from the taps in the bathtub while I ease out of my clothes. I catch sight of myself in the mirror. The bright lighting doesn't do me any favors. My hair is wild and ratty. My arms are filthy up to my elbows, caked with crusty, spoiled food that smells awful. My throat's starting to bruise, too. I lower myself into the steaming bathtub. Goose bumps flare across my skin, but the heat relaxes my tense muscles. I sink down to my neck and close my eyes.

It's dark when I wake up in bed, my hair still wet. I can hear Dad downstairs.

Stepping into the living room, I find him watching the Reports. He is on the sofa in the same place Mom always sat. He isn't sobbing like she would, or even panicking. He's just frowning at the screen.

He sees me standing in the doorway and flicks the TV off.

"You don't have to turn it off," I say.

"They were just covering what happened this afternoon in the sector. Apparently the New Worlders have been visiting the sectors that are closer to the end during the day to collect citizens. Never had a problem until now." He shrugs.

"Was anyone hurt?" I ask.

"The family made it to the New World okay, along with the four New Worlders that collected them."

"And the people from the sector?"

Dad shakes his head. "Three of them were killed."

I curl up on the sofa next to him. "I'm sorry for being there."

"I'm just glad it wasn't you." He drapes an arm around my shoulder and I rest my head on his chest.

"Dad?"

"Mm," he responds sleepily.

"Will you stay with me on the last day?"

He chokes. It takes him a moment to answer. "I'll be there for you, Sia."

My eyes warm with tears and I quirk my lips into a pathetic smile in response to his words.

10 DAYS

I'm alone.

Dad left me sleeping on the sofa. Jerking my head up, I leap from where I'm laying. The swiftness in which I jump up makes me dizzy and I can't move until the feeling passes.

Looking at the sofa, Mom's death comes flooding back. I can't understand why Dad would leave me here, lying where she lay, sleeping where she slept. Once my dizzy spell is over, I run up to my bedroom to change clothes.

There's a light tap at the front door just after 9:00 a.m. Mace.

On my way to answer, I check myself in the hall mirror. My neck's bruised, but that's the only visible evidence of what happened yesterday. What he won't see is my aching ribs and my black-and-blue legs. I open the door.

Mace stands on the stoop. The morning light shines behind him, framing his body. He grins at me and I get dizzy all over again.

"Hi," he says.

I invite him inside and lead him to the kitchen. "Have you eaten?" I ask.

"Not yet," he says.

"Me neither," I say and offer to make some breakfast.

I start clearing away empty dishes. Mace drags one of the wooden chairs out from under the table. He shrugs his jacket off—so that he's only wearing a plain black T-shirt, exposing his toned, tattooed arms, and black jeans—and drapes it over the back of the chair. Then he comes to stand beside me at the sink and dries the plates I wash.

"You really don't have to help, you know."

"I know," he says, continuing to dry. A smile tugs at my lips and I turn back to the soapy water.

He sits while I fix us something to eat. He insists on helping, but he doesn't know where anything is. It's much quicker if I do it. "You did well," he says as I open the cupboards. "At the store, I mean. You've got plenty to last."

"Yeah, just about. I was lucky," I say, turning to smile at him.

I toast a bagel for each of us. I'll only have one left after this but I don't mind. I butter them and pour two glasses of juice.

"Are you alone here?" Mace asks in between bites.

"Most of the time," I say, tracing lines in the condensation on the outside of my glass with my fingertip.

He frowns. "Who do you live with?"

"My dad, but he isn't around much." I don't mention my mom. I'm not ready to talk about that. I don't think I ever will be. Not in the short time I have left, anyway.

"You're okay, though, right?"

"I'm fine," I say, shrugging.

"Good." He wipes his mouth and pushes his empty plate forward so he can rest his elbows on the tabletop. "Look, Sia, about the other day. It was a total misunderstanding. I wasn't trying to get close to you *just* to recruit you."

I take a long drink of my orange juice.

"I can see why you'd think that," he continues. "I just want you to know that that isn't how it was meant to come across. You make me nervous, and I said all the wrong things—"

I choke.

"Are you okay?" he asks.

I pat at my chest. My eyes are watering. "*I* make *you* nervous?"

He nods slowly. "The more I get to know you, the more I don't want you to join us. I want to keep you safe." My cheeks and the tips of my ears burn red-hot. Mace watches me and grins. "Are we okay?"

I can't find words, so I nod. We're more than okay. I'm just glad he still wants to be around me. I find myself craving to be near him too, and I'm finally letting myself have what I want. I want to be with Mace. I want to fight. I want to live.

"Tell me more about your team," I say after a slight pause.

"We don't have to talk about that. It's fine if you don't want to join. Seriously. I still want to spend time with you."

My stomach cartwheels. "I might want to join," I say. "Maybe. I want to hear more about it first."

Mace smiles. "Why the change of heart?"

"Yesterday, when the sector rebelled, I needed you."

"It was mayhem. A lot of people got hurt," he says.

"I don't want to always need saving. If you're going to fight for your life, why shouldn't I? I guess I'm curious about what I can do other than, how did you put it? 'Stand there and let them kill me'."

He laughs a little. "That's good to hear."

"So, tell me more. I promise not to run away this time."

"Well, we're a small group at the moment and are looking for more to join. We just need to be careful about it."

"Because of the cameras?"

"Right. And if we ask the wrong person to join, they could report us."

"Right."

"Training sessions are scheduled once a day. We have weapons—tools, baseball bats, knives. Not great but they're the best we can do. And we have a couple of guns, but not a lot of ammunition, so we're selective about who will use them."

It's clear, from the amount of information he has, that Mace is high up in this group. Maybe even its leader. And he's one of the few trusted with a gun. If his team knew he'd been firing it to scare off thieves a few days ago, what would they think? I'm sure they'd be furious. Still, I smile internally. He must care to risk using what little ammunition he had to save me even though he'd only just met me.

"So, what happens if I say yes, that I want to join?" I ask.

"You'll come to the meeting tomorrow morning with me and start training."

"And what happens if I say no?"

"If you say no, I'll come and see you after training and we can hang out. If you want."

"Hmm," I tease. "I'm tempted by both."

Mace laughs. I already know what I'm going to say. This will be good for me. It gives me a chance to have some control, to be as safe as I possibly can be, and at least to have more purpose to my last few days.

"You better stop by in the morning and take me to the meeting, then," I say.

Mace stands and swoops down to give me a hug. I'm caught off-guard and my hands are pinned to my sides. He's crushing my ribs. "Um, ouch" is all I can say.

"Oh!" He moves back, still keeping his hands on my shoulders. "Did I hurt you?"

"It's okay," I say, smiling.

"You're really coming?"

"I really am."

Mace rubs my arms. "You have no idea how happy it makes me that you want to live. I promise I will protect you." He hugs me again, softer this time. Butterflies explode in my stomach, and I wrap my arms around him, molding my body with his.

"If I get good enough you won't need to," I say.

He lets go and pulls his chair closer to mine and sits again, holding on to my hand. "What do you want to do today? Are you up for going out?"

"Don't you have army duties to attend to?" I joke.

"Not until tomorrow morning. And if I did, you'd be coming with me, remember?" he says. "Come on, what'll it be?"

I think of my list, screwed up into a ball somewhere on my bedroom floor. Probably lost under a pile of clothes or rolled under the bed, but I'm ready to revisit it. "We could go swimming?"

Mace pulls a face.

"You know, in the lake," I say.

"For real?" he says. "You know that lake's dirty, right? Freezing, too."

I laugh and shrug my shoulders. "I've never been swimming. And I want to, before, you know . . ."

"Say no more. Swimming it is," Mace says. "One question: if you've never been swimming, how do you expect to swim?"

"Is there something I can take to float on?"

Mace thinks for a second and looks around the room. "You can hold on to me," he says. And there it is again: an assault of butterflies zigzagging around inside me, crashing into each other. "I'll keep you above the surface," he says. "I promise."

Our eyes lock.

"I trust you."

No one is at the lake. I saw some people sitting on the curbs outside their houses, gossiping about yesterday's riot and the deaths of the three citizens. I tuned them out. I want to forget for today.

Mace places the two towels I brought from home on the dry grass beside the lake and starts taking off his socks and shoes. I follow suit.

He removes his shirt, revealing his tattooed chest. His jeans are low on his hips and I trace the shape of his body with my eyes. The skin of his arms is completely covered with intricate patterns that start at his wrists and travel up his arms, over his shoulders, and spread out across his chest. His toned stomach is bare, ink-free, rising and sinking with each breath.

He's watching me, amused.

"Oh," I breathe when I realize. "I'm sorry, I—"

Mace laughs and saves me the embarrassment of finishing that sentence. He strides over to the water and I follow him. There are more tattoos on his back. Between his shoulder blades is a warped old-fashioned clock, which serves as part of a butterfly's body. I stare at it. Time and freedom, two things we don't have. I wonder where else his skin is inked.

Mace is only wearing jeans and I can see he's shivering a little. I'm still almost fully dressed, all but my socks, shoes, and jacket. I'm feeling the sharp chill in the air, too. Maybe this wasn't the best idea. I don't want us both to get sick and spend the next ten days in bed with stacks of tissues and hot drinks.

Mace plunges his bare foot into the water, rippling the surface. He sucks in a breath.

"That bad?" I ask.

"Mm," he says through gritted teeth, which I take to mean yes.

He lifts his foot out. I think he's changed his mind, until he jumps in, tucking his legs up to his chest, and disappears underwater.

"*Mace!*" I pace the edge of the water, waiting for him to come back up.

Moments later, his head crashes through the surface and he shakes it, sending drops of water flying in every direction. I let out a breath. "Are you okay?"

He swims toward the side of the lake, where I'm standing. "Never better," he says, his teeth chattering.

"It's freezing, isn't it?" I ask, backing up.

"Yep, but you can't back out now."

"But what if we get sick?"

"I'll get sick if you don't hurry up and get in here."

I dip my toes into the water, jerking them back out immediately. I don't know how Mace is coping being in there.

He places himself in front of me and turns his back to me. "Climb in and wrap your arms over my shoulders."

Though reluctant, I do as he says. The water stings, like shards of ice scratching my skin. Worst. Idea. Ever.

I hold tight, running my hands over his firm shoulders until they brush against his throat and meet just under his neck. My ribs hurt, but I soon forget once he starts swimming, taking me with him.

My jaw is chattering so violently that I think my teeth are going to shatter. But despite my numb body and fierce shivering, it feels amazing. My legs drag weightlessly behind me. All that empty space is beneath us and we aren't sinking. This is what I imagine flying to be like. I wouldn't be able to get enough of it. I'd join the birds and fly right over the sector's wall—far, far away.

Mace holds my arm and spins me around so that we are face-to-face. My hands are still looped around his neck, my fingers brushing against the bottom of his hair. We're inches apart. His warm breath clouds my cold face, heating my cheeks. "Sia?"

I close my eyes. "Mm?"

"I can't feel my toes."

Mace swims us to the edge, and we're both bitterly cold. He lifts me out first, then hauls himself out beside me. He grabs for our towels, wrapping the first one around my shoulders and rubbing my arms. I take over so he can dry himself off. He slips his T-shirt back on and hops from foot to foot while he puts on his socks and shoes.

I sit on the floor to pull on my boots. I feel better with my jacket covering me, but my wet clothes are grossly uncomfortable. My shirt clings to my skin and my jeans scratch against my legs.

"Come on," Mace says. "I'll take you home."

He carries our towels and wraps an arm around my shoulders. Suddenly I forget how cold I am. Suddenly I'm on fire.

The walk is too short, and we arrive back in front of my house before I even register what street we're on. I could have kept walking for hours.

The lights are on inside, so I know Dad's home. I open the door and he shouts, "Sia, is that you?"

"Yeah. I'll be in soon," I call back.

"Your dad?" Mace says.

"Yeah. I guess I better go before he comes out."

"Okay," he says, leaning forward to kiss me on the cheek, transferring the wet towels into my arms as he does. "Better take a hot bath to warm up."

"I will," I say and step through the door. I hear Dad's chair screech against the kitchen floor. I close the door and head up the stairs.

"What were you up to?" Dad asks.

"What do you mean?"

"Who were you talking to out there? Did you and Kyra make up?"

His question makes me feel guilty. Kyra would have liked to swim in the lake with me. She'd probably get along well with Mace, too.

"No. Just a new friend," I say.

"Why are you soaked?"

"Why are you asking so many questions?" I tease.

"Why aren't you answering them?" he says, reaching up to nudge me. I smirk and tap my nose. He narrows his eyes. "Seriously, Sia. What are you up to?"

"Seriously, Dad. Nothing. I went for a swim in the lake is all."

"It's freezing! Who were you there with? Was it some kind of party?"

"Not a party. Just a friend . . . from school." I'm not sure why I lie other than being afraid he won't approve, and I don't want him to put an end to this. Not now. He shakes his head and goes back into the kitchen.

I get the water running in the tub and shimmy out of my wet clothes. I head back into my room and hunt around on the floor for my list. I find it under a pile of T-shirts and smooth it out. I check off *1. Swim in the lake.*

I stare at the list. There's only one thing left on there: *4. Kiss a boy.* I think of Mace and a shy smile spreads across my lips as I stuff the paper to the back of my drawer.

9 DAYS

"Do you always do this?" I ask Mace.

We're walking together in a circle around the sector, winding through streets with no sense of direction.

"Pretty much, yeah. The cameras are still watching us, remember? You must always be aware of them."

"I am. But don't we look suspicious, walking around with no real purpose?"

"We'd look more suspicious if we were joined by twenty others heading straight to the high school."

He takes my hand when we reach the training facility, otherwise known as the abandoned high school. Everyone else has entered using different routes and different doors.

"I'm nervous," I say.

"Don't be," Mace says, brushing my hair out of my eyes.

I let go of Mace and shake my hands by my sides, like I can fling the worry away. He presses his palm on the small of my back and guides me toward the doors. I feel those familiar little sparks dance around beneath my skin wherever he touches me. Once inside, he links his fingers with mine and leads me down the hall.

The lights are out, and the early morning sun streaming through the small windows provides very little brightness. We walk in silence. My boots squeaking on the linoleum floor is the only sound in the building until we reach the double doors leading into the gym. I can hear voices on the other side.

"You okay?" Mace asks.

I swallow. "I think so."

With one shove, the doors are open and all heads turn to face us. The light in the gym is still a dull gray, but the windows lining the tops of the walls make it much brighter than the hallway. Keeping a good grip on my hand, Mace leads me toward the group, though I stay slightly hidden behind him.

"No," I hear, before we even make it halfway to them. Footsteps approach.

I don't look up. I'm too humiliated by the rejection. I only just got here. I'm good enough—I know I am—and I'll prove it to them. I want to be here.

I squeeze my eyes shut and prepare myself to step out from behind Mace.

"Len, stop," Mace says.

My eyes fly open. *Len?* That's my dad's name.

I peer around Mace's body, and there he is. Dad.

"Not her. Not this one," he says. "Mace, what were you thinking?"

"Len, she is perfectly capable—"

"She's my daughter, you idiot." Dad shoves Mace to the side and grabs me by the shoulders. "I will not allow it," he says. "You're sixteen!"

"Dad—" I look at the group. I'm mortified.

He turns around, notices the silence that surrounds us, the eyes that are on us. "Out here," he says, ordering me back into the hallway.

Dad uses both hands to slam through the double doors and I follow, narrowly missing them hitting me in the face as they swing back. So this is what he's been doing. This is where he's been. This is what he meant when he said he was doing all he could do to protect my mom and me from the machines. He's training to fight them.

Dad paces the corridor, his boots screeching each time he turns on his heel. His fist is practically in his mouth. He stops in front of me, turns, looks at me. "What are you doing here? What did he tell you?"

"He told me everything."

"Specifics, Sia. Come on."

"You're building your own army, and you're going to fight the machines," I say.

"Right. And did he tell you we're a really small group?"

"Yes."

"Did he tell you we have barely any decent weapons?"

"Yes."

Dad shakes his head. "I didn't want you to know about this."

"*Why?*"

"Has it given you hope? Knowing about us?"

I shrug. "I guess it has. Yes."

"That's why." He jabs his finger into my shoulder and then turns his back to me.

"Oh, that's nice," I say. "So you'd rather I spend the next nine days knowing I'm going to die than spend them hoping I'm going to live?"

He spins around. "Don't twist it, Sia. You know I want you to be happy. But I also want you to be safe, and fighting with us isn't safe."

"Nowhere is safe! I'm here because I want to be here. You can't change my mind."

"I don't have to let you in."

"I want to be part of it!" I yell, desperate now.

"Sia," Dad sighs, rubbing his hands over his face. "I don't want you here risking your life. It's no place for you."

"It's no place for any of us! I either leave now, alone, and wait to die. Or I join and I fight. Even if I still die, at least I *tried*. Please, Dad. Please give me that. I want to fight."

His face is scrunched up. "I want to fight *for* you. Not alongside you. I want to protect you."

My eyes warm. "I know, Dad. But I can't sit at home doing nothing now that I know you're here and that this group exists." I pause, wait. "Please let me stay," I whisper.

His face relaxes and he pulls me into his arms. I suck in a breath, my ribs still tender, and crush my face against his chest. "It's dangerous," he says.

"It's dangerous no matter where I am," I say, letting go of his embrace. "Whatever I do, I'm probably going to die. At least if I join this group I can spend the time with you . . . and Mace."

Dad's mouth quirks up slightly on one side. "Your new friend?"

I blush, then nod. "Who knows, we might even win. Or, I'll die alongside you and the others, rather than at home on my own."

Dad places his arm around my shoulder, squeezes me tight, and leads me back into the gym. Everyone stops chattering and looks up. Mace is standing beside a boy with shocking white-blonde hair. Dad introduces me to the group.

"Everybody, this is Sia. My daughter."

I'm greeted by a mumbled chorus of "Hi Sia," then I take a seat on a bench beside Mace. He takes my hand and squeezes it.

Dad remains standing and silences the group. I guess I was wrong about Mace being the leader. I take a moment to look around at everyone and spot a boy from my year in school. I don't think I've ever spoken to him. I don't think he really spoke to anybody. I see other men, some of my dad's friends, and boys—their sons?

My eyes find a girl with dark wavy hair and a firm expression. She looks tough. When her eyes flick to me, I avert my gaze. I count twenty-four men, women, girls, and boys that make up this group. *It's not enough.* We're a community of four hundred and sixteen. Subtract the families who've gone to the New World and the ones who can't fight, and you're still left with over one hundred people. Where are they all?

Some look strong, some don't. Some look fearless, some look afraid. But they clearly all have hope. I can see it in their eyes—a spark of determination. It's something I haven't seen in many since the clock started counting down. *Is this what Mace saw in me?*

"Okay, let's get started," Dad says. "For those of you that have just joined us, I'll quickly recap before beginning today's session. All of you are here to fight against the machines that will land in this sector in nine days. As we don't have a lot of information about the cyborgs, it can be difficult to know exactly what to train for.

"As most of you know, we're working to find out more about the machines from one of our own that was recently taken to the New World. He has not been in touch, but we always knew it was a long shot.

"So, as it stands, we've put together an assortment of tasks that we feel will be of use. During training session you'll be expected to exercise—keeping our fitness at a high standard is important. We also offer reflex training, work on aim, and practice fighting skills.

"Today we'll start with a thirty-minute warm-up, then we'll move on to fight training. And for those who joined recently, you will catch up—training exercises are always repeated. Now, split into groups of four and warm up."

I'm with Mace, the blonde guy, and the scary girl that caught me studying her earlier.

"Hi," she says when we're all together. "I'm Cass."

Maybe she's not so scary after all. "Sia," I say.

"How come you're only joining us now? Your dad put this whole thing together, so what's kept you from coming?"

"He didn't tell me about it," I mutter, embarrassed.

"What? No way. That sucks!"

I'm so humiliated. "It does."

"Sure he had his reasons, right? Come on, we're on laps," she says, slapping my arm and taking off jogging around the gym.

I rub the place where she hit me.

"Cass wasn't giving you a hard time, was she?" Mace asks.

"No, she was fine. So we should . . ." I use my thumb to point over my shoulder. Cass and the blonde guy are already on their second lap.

We start jogging side by side. "Why didn't you tell me that Len was your dad?" he asks.

"Why would I? I didn't know you knew him. Everyone apparently knows him better than I do." We turn a corner and I see Dad watching us from the side, his thumb pressed against his lips.

"He didn't tell you anything? Why? He recruited me. He started all of this."

"So people keep telling me."

"You're saying he kept it all a secret from you?" Mace says.

"Yep. Can we just train now?" I'm feeling stupider and stupider the longer this conversation stretches—the leader's daughter who knew nothing about her father's group of rebels.

"After warm-up." We stop to stretch. "Don't worry about your dad. I'm sure he had his reasons."

"Yeah. That's what Cass said."

The morning flies.

I learned that the group trains from 7:00 a.m. to 9:00 a.m., then 10:00 a.m. to 12:00 p.m. We had a break at nine, but I worked through it, determined to catch up. Mace says the hours have become more irregular now, though. The closer we get, the longer the hours. Dad just tells the group what time to meet, and we finish when we finish.

We move on to fighting skills in the afternoon. I've never done anything like this before, but I'm better at it than I thought I would be. I'm pitted against Cass. She's fierce and never slows. I jump left and right, dodge her, and avoid what would have been some pretty nasty blows. I even get one in myself, winding her. I try not to smile when she doubles over, clutching her stomach.

It doesn't seem like long before Dad dismisses us, instructing everyone to meet back tomorrow morning to resume training. I check the clock on the wall and see that it's 2:00 p.m. I haven't stopped for seven hours.

Dad makes his way over to my group. He sees Cass on the bench behind me with her head on her lap. "Everything all right, Cass?" he says.

"It would be if your psycho daughter hadn't punched me so hard."

Dad glances at me for a second then turns back to Cass. "Maybe we should focus on reflexes more with you, then." She scowls, stands, and leaves. "She has a vicious temper," he whispers to me.

I smirk, admittedly feeling a little smug. "I noticed."

He turns and calls Mace over.

"Len, I'm sorry I—"

Dad raises his hands. "It's me who should be apologizing. It was a shock seeing you bring my daughter here to join our army, but that doesn't excuse my behavior. You didn't know."

Mace nods.

"So, Sia, how did you find things today?" Dad asks, turning his attention back to me.

"I think it went well."

"It was better than that," Mace says. "She dodged most of Cass's hits and punched her so hard in the gut that Cass couldn't get back up."

"A machine will get back up, though," Dad reminds me. "Still, it's good to hear you're doing well. Just don't think that by injuring the human body that you're getting the upper hand—what's coming for us isn't human."

"Yeah, I know."

Dad scruffs up my hair. "Proud of you, Sia. I'll see you two back home once I'm finished here."

Mace insists on preparing lunch for the two of us when we get home. I don't argue.

He makes a cup of hot tea for me, with an extra spoonful of sugar. I need something sweet.

Dad's speech at the gym has stuck with me—the part about not knowing enough about the machines to really train to fight them properly. Sure, what we're doing is all right, but how can we prepare properly if we don't know what's coming? And who was supposed to be his source from the New World? How could they possibly communicate without it being tracked?

Mace waves a hand in front of my eyes. "Earth to Sia."

"What? Did you say something?"

"I asked you if you enjoyed today."

"Oh. Right. Yeah, I did. I liked it a lot."

"Even the parts that didn't involve punching Cass?" he says. I laugh, and he joins in. "You seemed to settle in well. You're a quick learner."

My mind drifts back to the gym, to our source in the New World, to the cyborgs we know nothing about. It's all so frustrating. I'm sure there aren't enough of us. And six sectors have fallen already.

There were no survivors.

Surely others tried to fight. I wonder if too much hope is being put into this group. I'm desperate to do more, to help, to find the answers.

There is one thing I could do. It came to me during warm-up, but I'm not even sure it's possible. The danger and the possibility of something going wrong is too high. It's a huge risk. I shouldn't even be considering it. I can't tell Dad or Mace. They would put a stop to it right away.

No, I need to speak to Lilly. She's the only one who can help me.

Mace and I eat lunch without hardly speaking. He clutches at conversation here and there but it doesn't go far. He leaves once we finish, and I'm not even sure that I say goodbye.

Dad arrives home not long after. I'm still at the table, scratching at the wooden surface with my bitten nails. Dad sits across from me. "Well, now you know."

"Yep, I guess I do," I say. "I felt pretty stupid at the meeting today when everyone realized how clueless I was."

"Sia, I didn't want you to know. I knew you'd want to join if I told you and I wanted to protect you, not have you fighting."

I sigh. We're just stomping over old ground. "You should have told me, Dad. Mace said he saw something special in me when we met. Do you not see anything special in me? I know you didn't want me to fight, but did it not cross your mind that I might be good at it?"

"That's not fair. I see more in you than you'll ever know. You're so special, so extraordinary. Don't doubt for a second that I don't see that part of you just because I didn't ask you to join my army. It's because you're so special to me that I didn't."

"I'm obviously not that special," I mumble, crossing my arms across my chest.

"And why do you think that?"

"If I was, I'd have been asked to join the New World."

Dad's eyes narrow. "And you think that their idea of special is the right one? You trust their judgments?"

"No, I guess not. I've got a lot on my mind, and there's so much I don't understand."

"Neither do I, Sia," Dad sighs. "Neither do I."

109

8 DAYS

I wait for the shutters to unlock.

I can't sleep. There's too much on my mind. I can't stop thinking about seeing Lilly. At 4:00 a.m. I give up trying to sleep and wait for curfew to be lifted, shutters to be opened, to be free to leave this house.

I'm dressed and ready when 6:00 a.m. comes and the metal shutters groan as they rise. I hurry to beat Dad out of the house, locking my bedroom door from the outside by slipping a hairclip through the hole and sliding the lock to the side.

I stop in the kitchen. Even though there's no way I can eat, I pack up a few things for Lilly. I leave Dad a note on the fridge. I write that I'm too sore to train and need to rest up for a day, which is fair seeing how badly I've been beaten over the past few days.

Mace will be here in a couple hours to go to the high school together, so I stick a note to the front door, too, saying more or less the same thing. With two fruit juices and a handful of snack bars in my backpack, I grab my old, scuffed boots from beside the front door and slip out before Dad catches me. I've got one boot on, and I hop down the driveway while I pull on the other.

Once I reach the hill, I climb at top speed, stumbling all the way until I find Lilly's camp.

"Hi," she says. "You're back."

"Yep. And that's not all," I say, emptying the food out onto the ground. "Hungry?"

She claps her hands and grabs a snack bar. I feel bad for not coming sooner, and for only coming, really, because I want something from her. Lilly demolishes the bar in two big bites. She tears off the lid to the fruit juice and drinks it down in one long gulp. Then she grabs for the other. I laugh. "Slow down! You'll make yourself sick!"

She giggles and, using her torn sleeves, wipes the purple liquid from around her mouth. "So was it your friend?" she asks.

"What?"

"The aircraft. Did they take your friend? Was her family chosen like you thought?" She opens another snack bar.

"Oh, no. It was for a teacher from the high school. A family of five."

"I'm sorry," she says, with her mouth full. "Which teacher was it?"

"It was Mr. Elvin and his family."

Lilly nods, swallows. "That makes sense."

"You know them?"

"Of course. Everyone had at least one class with Mr. Elvin. I had classes with Mrs. Elvin, too. They're nice."

"I never saw you at school," I say.

"I saw you there, sometimes. That was only because Finn had a crush on you."

I feel my face redden and I laugh to cover my discomfort. I think hard and remember Finn. He and I had some classes together, but we didn't really speak much.

Lilly and I make our way to the top of the hill while we chat. When we sit down, I start tugging on the long, brittle grass, pulling it out of the ground and flinging it to the side.

I'm working up my nerve to tell Lilly my plan, but am having a hard time finding the words even though I spent all night running over exactly what I was going to say.

"Lilly, I have something I want to speak to you about," I start. She looks at me, waiting. I take a deep breath. "I'm not really supposed to tell you this."

Lilly shrugs. "Who am I going to tell?"

"No one, I guess. But it is secret and you have to keep it that way."

She laughs. "Sia, you're the only person I've spoken to in over a week."

"I know, Lilly, but this is serious. I joined a group. They're—*we're*—training to fight against the machines when they get here."

She sniggers. "That's so stupid!"

"Lilly!"

"Well it is! You should just come and stay up here with me like I keep telling you. Fighting seems kind of pointless, don't you think?"

"So does hiding," I counter, then feel bad about it. "I mean, don't you think the people in the other sectors tried to hide? Nobody survived. We'd all hide if it were that simple."

"And don't *you* think the people in the other sectors tried to fight? Of course they must have." She crosses her arms, anger in her tone.

"I didn't say they hadn't. But this is different."

"Fighting is pointless," Lilly scoffs. "Even if the people in the other sectors tried, it didn't work. They're all dead."

"That doesn't mean our fate will be the same. I have this idea, something that could put us ahead, something that could help the sector gain its chance of survival. I think if we knew more about the machines—how they attack, how they're activated, how they work—then we might have a better chance of beating them. Right now we don't even know what they look like. We've no idea what we're up against."

"Exactly. That's why fighting will get you nowhere— you don't know what you're fighting."

"But what if we did?"

"What do you mean?"

"I think I know how I can get to the New World and find out more, but the plan needs *you* in order to work." I hold my breath and wait for her reaction.

"Sia, you're insane! You know that, right?"

Not what I was hoping for. "Just hear me out. Please," I beg.

Lilly laughs and shakes her head. "I think I've heard enough of your plan to get us both killed."

"You really think I'd do that? I'm not looking to get us killed. I've thought about this, and it could work."

"Could work, huh? Convincing. And where do I come into all of this?"

"Well, I'd need you to take me to your house in the sector."

"I can't go down there," she says. "Plan over. They'll see me on the cameras."

"I already thought of that. We can avoid the cameras, and I brought you a hat and scarf as a disguise."

Lilly rolls her eyes. "They aren't going to fall for a disguise. Besides, it isn't even that cold out!"

"It's cold enough," I say. "When we get to your house, I want to send a message to the New World that I'm you. I'll tell them that I was left behind, that I've changed my mind, that I want to be with my family. They'll come for me and take me to the New World. Then I'll find out what I can while I'm there."

Lilly's face screws up and her eyes shine with tears at the mention of her family. "Then what?" she says.

"Then you call them and turn me in. You tell them there was a mistake, that I took the leaflet from you and went in your place. They'll come for you while they're looking for me, but I'll already be on the aircraft, hidden, waiting to be brought home."

"So I'd have to go to the New World? For good?"

"I know it's a lot to ask."

Lilly gets to her feet. "A lot to ask? Sia, you're asking me to go against everything I stand for! You know I hate the idea of that place. You know I ran away from my family to avoid going there. What makes you think I'd do this for you? I don't even know you."

She turns and storms away from me, crashing through the bushes, disappearing. My heart is hammering in my chest. *What now?* I don't have a plan B. Lilly was it—my only chance.

I lie back. The soft wind gently caresses my face, lulling me to sleep. I don't want to go back down to the sector. Not yet. My eyes sting, begging me to close them after staying awake most of the night. I let the wind carry me far, far away.

There are two hands on my shoulders, shaking me awake. Two blue eyes blinking back at me. The sky is blocked by Lilly's face. She lets go and steps back. The late morning light irritates my eyes. I rub them.

"What are you *doing*?" I croak.

"I'm in," she says.

"What?"

"I'm in, I said. On board. Whatever you want to call it. Let's go." She pulls me to my feet. I brush at the grass that clings to my jeans.

"Why did you change your mind?"

"You can't do this without me. And, if I go to the New World this way, at least I'll be going for the right reason," she says. "I guess I don't have anything to lose, right?"

We arrive at Lilly's house.

I think I made it through the sector without being spotted by anyone who might have recognized me. I want Dad and Mace to believe I'm in bed. I feel sick keeping this from them. What if something goes wrong and I can't get back? What if I never see them again?

I shake my head, flinging away my doubts. I can't think like that. I will come back. I will see them both again.

Lilly's house looks exactly like mine, inside and out. But there's a piano in the corner of the living room. That's different. The stool isn't tucked in and there's a half-empty mug on the coffee table. Her family must have left in a hurry.

The house smells musty, abandoned. There's an eerie atmosphere, as if Lilly's family died and no one has come by since. I shudder.

Lilly disappears into the kitchen, leaving me standing in the hallway and peering into the living room. She reemerges moments later holding an electronic device against her chest.

"Okay. Are you ready to do this?" she says. "This is your last chance to back out."

I'm not sure that I am ready but say, "I'm not backing out. Are *you* sure about this?"

She nods, takes a deep breath, and turns the device on. Lilly presses a button, then shoves it into my hands. It searches for connection and we wait in silence for someone to answer on the other end—in the New World.

"Greetings! How may I be of assistance today?"

I clear my throat. "My name is Lilly Tanner," I say. "There has been a mistake. My family is in the New World, and I've been left behind in the sector." Lilly's eyes fill up and I look away from her. It takes a moment for the voice to respond. I start to think the connection's been lost.

"Oh you poor, poor dear!" The cheery voice returns, startling me. *"You must be terrified, all alone in that place. Well, don't you worry for one second, I will send out an aircraft to collect you. I just need you to do one teeny thing before I do that, okay?"*

"Sure," I say, looking nervously back at Lilly.

"Great! On your screen you will see a small rectangular box on the right hand side. Do you see it, my dear?"

"I see it."

"Wonderful! Now, Lilly, I'll be needing you to press your thumb down inside the box to take a quick scan. Can you do that for me?"

Lilly reaches over and presses her thumb into the box on the screen. It lights up for a couple of seconds, then the screen flashes green and displays one word: ACCEPTED.

"Excellent, Lilly! Thank you for your cooperation, dear. Now, you hang in there, sweetie. The aircraft will arrive after curfew, at 1:00 a.m. Be ready to board immediately."

"I will," I say.

"You hold on tight, sweetheart. We'll be there to get you in no time," she says, then the call cuts off.

The screen is still flashing green in acceptance to Lilly's thumbprint. She takes it from me and switches it off.

"What do we do now?" I ask.

Lilly goes into the living room and I follow. "Wait," she says, flopping onto the sofa. I sit beside her and she kicks her feet up onto my lap. "And hope that we'll both be okay."

"We will be," I say. *We have to be.*

While Lilly sleeps I have time to think.

I've seen the New World on TV, but I can still hardly imagine what it'll be like when I get there. To be in a place where the tiniest slip-up could cost me my life. *You wanted purpose*, I remind myself. *You chose to do this.*

The plan is good. Lilly wouldn't have agreed to it if it wasn't. Her legs are still across my lap and I lean forward to grab the remote from the coffee table, careful not to disturb her. I switch the TV on and press mute.

The Reports are playing a video loop—the same one that's on between the news. They show the sectors first—the streets and houses from different angles, children in school classrooms, workers in factories. Then comes the New World—its streets and houses, a thriving commercial area, the school classrooms, and robots working in the factories. Everything's clearly portrayed as being "better."

Lilly rolls over and opens her eyes. She frowns when she looks at the screen. "Turn it off. I don't want to see."

I do as she says.

She leaves the room and doesn't take the electronic leaflet with her, so I switch it on and look at the menu. There's a profile on her family. I click it open. There's an image of her mom and one of her dad joined together by a line. Below are three empty boxes where photographs should be. Lilly's name is in the first one. I press the box.

There's little information on Lilly. Nothing more than her name, her date of birth, and what she may or may not have inherited from her parents.

Lilly returns and gasps. "Sia, you'll drain the battery!" She takes the device from me and switches it off. "I need this to report you. Don't turn it on again. What were you looking at, anyway?"

"I only saw the images of your parents, then clicked on your name. There was nothing really there. I thought it might have been good if I knew a bit more about you and your family before I get to the New World."

"Well, you can just ask me if you are so curious."

We spend the afternoon going over the details of Lilly's life. She tests me on all sorts of tidbits that may not even matter and before long it's dark out and there's only a couple of hours left until the New World aircraft arrives.

"What do you think?" she says. "Are you ready to be me?"

"I hope so."

7 DAYS

I can't relax.

Lilly's sleeping so comfortably here in the house she shared with her family. The same family that left her here to die.

The living room reminds me of my mom. I try to relax but I can't, so I head into the kitchen. It's after midnight now, but the shutters are still up. This house doesn't fall under curfew like the rest tonight.

I sit at the kitchen table, drumming my fingers on the surface and watching the clock. Time slithers on painfully slow.

It's almost 1:00 a.m. I feel hot, *too hot*. I go to the sink to fill a glass with cold water, but the water's shut off. I run up to the second floor and try the bathroom, but I have no luck there, either. I try the lights and find the electricity is off now, too.

I go into a bedroom, one that faces the front of the house, so I can watch for the aircraft. There are two twin beds pushed up against opposite walls. They're unmade. Drawers are open, clothes hanging out of them. A doll lies at a crooked angle by the door. I look out of the window, and wait.

1:00 a.m. comes and goes. I give up at the window and head back downstairs. I pace around the kitchen, restless and tired. I check the clock over and over, starting to doubt that it even works properly.

2:00 a.m. Something's wrong. *They aren't coming.* Still, I wait.

3:00 a.m. I sit at the kitchen table with my head resting in my hands. I drift in and out of sleep, trying to catch myself when I doze off.

4:00 a.m. There's a light tap at the door. My heart leaps.

I walk along the hallway and close the door to the living room so they can't see Lilly, then take a deep breath and open the front door.

"Miss Tanner?" the men say in unison—two New Worlders, dressed head-to-toe in black and armed to the teeth.

I nod, not trusting myself to speak. They step to the side and motion me out of the house. I follow them around the house to the black-as-night aircraft waiting for me around back. I suck in a breath. *This is it.*

They open the doors and I turn to look back at the sector. I start to whisper goodbye to the place, just in case, but I catch myself. *Stop it. I'm coming back.* This isn't goodbye.

"Climb aboard, Miss Tanner."

I step inside and scan the interior for places to hide on the way back. There are plenty of storage boxes lined up against the sides. There are six metal seats, three per row in the middle, with safety belts that make an X shape across them.

There's a small exit door on the side. The pilot area has a door on either side, too, that opens upward instead. Three ways in, three ways out.

We take off. My stomach turns upside-down as we climb into the night sky and I leave the sector for the first time ever.

An eternity goes by.

Or that's how it feels, anyway. I don't actually know how long we've been in the air. The New Worlders haven't spoken to me again so far.

I sit in the middle of the back row of seats with the safety belts across my body, pinning me down to the cold metal chair. Up so high in the air, I'm afraid we might fall. I'll die if we crash; I'll die if I'm found out. So many things could go wrong today. My stomach is in knots while I wait to arrive in the New World. It can't be much longer.

We start to dip and my insides roll over and over. Suddenly, the pressure in my ears is too much to bear. I clamp my hands over them but it does nothing. *What's happening?* I squeeze my eyes shut and wait for it to stop.

Finally, we land. I unclip the safety belt and step out of the aircraft when I'm told. I'm glad to be back on solid ground, but terrified of what awaits me next. My ears still throb, but I can hear better now.

I'm standing on a long strip of smooth, black tarmac. The New Worlders point the way and walk on either side of me toward the city.

It's only just getting light out. In front of me is an enormous structure made of concrete, glass, and metal. It climbs so high, layer upon layer, floor stacked upon floor. It's all angles and windows, jutting out and bustling with activity. From all the way out here I can hear voices and laughter, see people moving around up there in their new homes.

And their view? I turn around.

Behind me, where the black tarmac strip ends, is the Rough. No walls, no gray, no barrier. One of the New Worlders touches my arm and suggests we keep walking. I do as he says.

Neon blue lines of light streak from one pillar to another in front of the New World. Behind them, a woman is waiting for me.

"What's that?" I ask.

"The gate," one of the New Worlders says in a gruff voice.

"How does it work?"

"They're lasers," he says, looking to the other and smirking. "If anyone tries to go through it'll floor them with a nasty shock and trip the alarms."

"Wow," I breathe.

The guard fishes a small disc from his pocket and slides his finger across it. The blue lines vanish. I can see the woman better now that she's no longer shielded by the gate. She's smartly dressed and holding an electronic note board out in front of her. She glances at it as I approach.

"Ah! Lilly Tanner!" she says, her voice brimming with delight. "Welcome to your new home!"

Her voice isn't what I expect. She's so cheerful and energetic. Giddy, even. Though her posture is stiff and her body language is cold, what comes out of her mouth is the opposite.

"We spoke earlier, dear. It's nice to meet you in person." She holds out a gloved hand and I take it. We shake. "I'm Felicity." She smiles, lines crack her cheeks, and I get the impression she doesn't smile too often.

She has dull red hair, with a thick gray streak on either side of her middle part. It's pulled back into a low, neat bun and smoothed down to perfection. Her face is angular. Her sharp features make her seem intimidating, masking her bubbly personality.

I still haven't spoken. Felicity continues, "We're delighted that you decided to join us. Your parents, in particular, are thrilled. They're waiting for you in your new house. But before you can join them, I must guide you through orientation. All right, muffin?"

"Sure," I say. I try to breathe normally. I don't know what to expect, but all I can do is go along with her and hope I can escape at some point to look for the machines on my own. *Before* she takes me to Lilly's new house.

"Splendid! Come along, then. We'll get you ready to start your new life with us."

I hear a sharp buzz behind me and turn to see the gate has been reactivated. I swallow, wondering how bad the shock would be if I ran through it. It could be my only option later.

Felicity leads me into the New World, through the entrance at the bottom of the city. The interior is just as spectacular as the exterior. The walls and floors are pure white and the ceilings are high. It looks new, fresh, how you'd expect the future to look.

In front of us are four escalators—two up, two down—and a glass elevator in between them.

"We'll take the elevator," Felicity says, pulling her glove off and pressing the call button. It glides noiselessly down to our level and pings open.

Felicity steps inside and I follow. We stop three floors up and step out into a gloomy, dark walkway. Not what I was expecting at all. We walk together through a long tunnel, and the lights flicker overhead.

Felicity sighs. "You'll have to excuse these parts. They're not quite finished yet."

"The city isn't finished?"

"No, dear, not just yet. Don't worry. The residential area is complete, so none of this will disrupt you. We're fully prepared to have our citizens move in and settle down."

"Where will I be living?" I ask.

"Up top, darling. The first few floors are maintenance. Middle floors are commercial: your stores and restaurants. Up top are the residential floors. You'll see all of that today, pumpkin."

"Are there other places like this?"

"Not yet, dear. Isn't it an honor to be part of the very first one? We're entering a new time, and this is where it begins." She squeals a little and claps her hands. "It's just marvelous!"

We come out of the tunnel into another enormous expanse of blinding white. White tiled floors against white tiled walls. White desks line either side of the room, with workers dressed in white tapping away on white computer keyboards.

The back wall is made up entirely of miniature televisions. My heart skips when I see the sectors on the screens. The other walls have images and citizen profiles projected onto them like the ones on the electronic device at Lilly's house. Potential residents?

There are more tunnels leading off in different directions. This room is like the center of a maze. Felicity looks at me and raises her eyebrows, as if she's waiting for some sort of reaction from me.

"Impressive," I say.

"Isn't it? This is where we'll spend our morning before heading up for the tour," she says. Felicity points to the wall on our left. "That leads to the staff cafeteria, where we'll eat today." She points to the wall on our right. "That leads to where the Reports are aired and controlled." I swallow the bile that rises in my throat. The people responsible for my mom's death are just through the door over there. Not just in that one room, though, but all around me. I clench my fists by my side. "Ahead to your left leads to Damien's office. You don't go down there unless you have an appointment. But why would you?" she says with a tinkling laugh. Then she points to the other tunnel on the right side of the back wall. "And that is where we'll be doing your orientation, sugar. Don't get lost, and stay with me at all times, okay?"

"Okay."

In a daze, I follow Felicity to the back wall and under an archway. Her thin heels click against the floor tiles.

After passing under the archway, I expect a dark corridor like the last, but this one is finished. The white tiled décor continues, but projected on the walls are trees with birds flying between the branches and soaring across the projected blue sky above my head. I walk on forest floor, patches of grass and flowers beneath my feet, even a clear stream that doesn't wet my shoes when I step into it.

I almost walk into Felicity when she stops before an open door that leads into a small, dark room.

"Someone's distracted, I see," she chirps. "It's no surprise. This is possibly my favorite corridor."

"What are the others like?" I ask, annoyed at how genuinely interested I am. I don't *want* to like anything about this place.

"Now, now," she says, wagging her finger. "That'll ruin the surprise. You'll pass through many ever-changing corridors during your time here. It really is technology at its best. You'd never see anything like this in your old sector, would you?"

I shake my head.

"There are a few that are quite spectacular. Of course, not every corridor is this advanced, but we hope to get there soon. Remember, we're a work in progress. You'll have to bear with us."

Felicity ushers me into the dark room. The lights flash on once I step inside.

There's nothing in here but a stool and a projector, like the ones we use in school. "Take a seat, muffin," Felicity says, pointing at the small metal stool. The room holds none of the luxury of the rooms leading up to it. It's more on par with the gloomy, unfinished tunnel we passed through earlier.

There's a crackling sound, then the wall in front of me lights up.

"Ahh, there we go!" Felicity says. She steps in front of the screen. Her shadow stretches up the wall behind, as if a monster is creeping up on her. "We're ready to begin! You're required to watch this short film, which will help you understand a little more what we're about here in the New World. Are you sitting comfortably, sweet?"

No. "Yes."

"Okay, then! Let's begin!" She presses play then switches out the lights and leaves the room.

She's gone? So soon? I didn't expect my opportunity to be alone to come so fast. But I haven't seen enough. I don't know where to go. She did say the first three levels are maintenance, middle is commercial, and top is residential. From that I assume the cyborgs are somewhere on one of the first three floors.

Loud music bounces off the four walls. The screen flashes images of the New World and happy families. Everyone's happy, everyone's smiling, everything's perfect.

I stand and head for the door. Gently easing the handle down until it clicks, I slowly pull the door toward me and peer through the gap. I can hear voices. *Damn.*

I pull it open a little more. Felicity has her back to me; she's talking to someone but I can't see the other person's face. Quietly, I close the door and return to my stool. I should have known it was too good to be true.

The music fades out. The screen goes blank for a split second, then Damien Hoist appears.

His hair is gelled firmly in place. His tanned skin glows, and his white teeth shine. They're perfectly straight and even. Everything about him is, right down to the last button on his lavish pinstripe suit. Not a crease in place, not a collar upturned or a shirt untucked. He oozes confidence.

"Welcome, newcomer," he says. "Let me be the first to congratulate you. You were chosen because you're special. You stand out to us. You have something that puts you above others and makes you a better person. And that is why you are here."

He flashes a wide smile at the camera. "You see, the New World welcomes only the most extraordinary people. We celebrate your uniqueness and your important role in society. We separate the stunningly beautiful from the average and unattractive, the budding athletic from the lazy and unfit, the intelligent from the unintelligent, the brave from the cowards, and so on.

"All of this can only benefit us and our world. We're moving forward, looking to our future, and I'm delighted to welcome you"—he points to the screen, right at me—"as a vital part of this movement."

Felicity comes back into the room and stands at the back. Damien continues his hideous welcome speech. "I looked at our sectors, and I was disappointed by what I saw. The authorities were caring for these people and getting very little in return. It's now time to start again and do things right. We are a new age. A new beginning. A New World."

The video cuts out. Felicity flicks the lights back on. "Isn't he *wonderful!*"

"Quite," I say.

She looks at her electronic pad, scrolling through it. "Ah, here we go. This should help you remember."

"Remember what?"

"What Damien is trying to teach you in his video."

"I already understand."

"Come on, dear. Cooperate! I have to check off all the points with you or you don't complete orientation. I have to run you through this exercise to make sure you know why you're here. Tell me what you know."

"My parents are musicians. So I guess that's why they were chosen and brought here." I shrug.

"Yes, and . . .?"

"And the New World celebrates, um, people who are better than everyone else."

"No, not *everyone* else. Just those left behind. Think about it this way. The sectors are pretty useless. Agreed?"

I force myself to nod.

"The people in the sectors are like pets. The authorities care for them, but they give nothing back. It's like they're sitting in a cage, getting on with their day, showing their owners no love, but the owner still has to care for them and clean them and feed them." I cross my arms and wonder how many times she's used this example. "Do you see what I'm saying? That's just what the people left behind in the sectors are like. Useless. They give nothing back. They're nothing to be proud of. Their lives are nothing. They *do* nothing. The New World, *this*, is everything."

Inside, I'm begging her to stop. "I understand," I say through gritted teeth. I understand that Damien loves himself, and clearly the deluded people living here love him, too.

What I don't understand is how a man who harbors so much hate and disregard for human life can be loved by so many. How does he gain this hold over people, so they believe his twisted ideas are the answer to everything that is wrong with the world?

Still sitting on the stool, one leg crossed over the other, I tap my foot on the floor. Felicity watches my foot *tap, tap, tap*, then checks her watch. "Time for some breakfast, I think," she says, opening the door and motioning for me to leave the room.

We head back into the woodland corridor and into the main white room. The workers are leaving their desks and heading to get some breakfast as well. I try to remember where each corridor leads so I can explore them later.

We enter the all-white cafeteria. Felicity walks straight to the front of the line, passing all the hungry workers who are lined up waiting patiently for their breakfast. I guess there's a lot to do at the moment, what with building the New World and scheduling the slaughter of those left behind in the sectors. *Must be tiring for them*, I think angrily.

"What would you like to eat, kitten?" Felicity asks once we reach the front of the line. I glance back at the workers behind us, my face burning.

"Um, I like pancakes. And porridge. Anything with syrup."

"Oh, yum! Two stack of pancakes and syrup," she orders.

We take a seat together in a far corner. No one sits near us. I don't speak, but Felicity says enough for the two of us. I nod along and pick at my pancakes. Why did I say pancakes? The smell takes me back to the morning I found Mom. I can't eat them. I don't think I could even hold anything down at the moment. It feels wrong sitting in their cafeteria, eating their food, pretending that I belong.

I worry about how long the orientation is taking. Lilly's call to report me hangs over me, the time drawing closer and closer. "What's next?" I ask Felicity, probably cutting her off mid-sentence, I'm not sure.

She doesn't seem to mind either way. "Next is the tour!" she says, clapping her hands like she did earlier. It doesn't suit her.

"Shall we go now?" I say, trying to hurry her along. I can't stop her giving me the tour, but I can certainly try to speed her up.

"Oh, someone's antsy." She giggles. Again, it doesn't suit her. "We can go once you're done eating."

"I'm done."

"But you haven't finished. In fact, you've hardly touched it at all."

"I'm too excited to eat," I lie.

She shakes her head. "Oh, very well."

We head back to the glass elevator and take it up to the top—the residential area.

Out of the elevator, we head through more projected corridors. Not all have projections yet. The ones without are spotless white walls, floors, and ceilings. It's hard to tell where the floor ends and the walls begin. It reminds me of the nonstop gray of the sector back home, and how everything kind of blends together. I run my fingertips along the smooth tiles and imagine what'll be projected onto these walls.

We walk through more forest projections. Tall, thick tree trunks surround us. Running water glitters in the sunlight. Birds sing and flowers bloom in every color you could dream up.

We go underwater. Bubbles swirl and pop around us. Tropical fish are everywhere. They circle us, but swim away when I put my hand up to them.

We pass through the dry sands of a desert, under a blistering sun, though I feel none of the piercing heat.

The projections seem so real. I've only ever seen images of places like these in school. Seeing this now makes me want to explore every aspect of the New World. It makes me wish I had more time—days, weeks, even years.

This place is evil, but it'd be a shame not to enjoy it, even just for a little while.

We step out into a courtyard. The houses climb up, up, up, like they're spiraling into the clouds above. They're all different shapes and sizes. This place is the opposite of back home, where all we have is flat land and rows of identical houses. Here they're scattered everywhere, in no order and all different colors—pinks, purples, blues, greens. Small trees in little gardens cast shadows on the footpaths. Sprinklers catch the sunlight, making small rainbows.

I catch myself staring, mouth ajar, when Felicity chuckles. "Look at you!" she says. "Lost for words! Astonishing, isn't it?"

"Yes," I say, and it's the truth. It is astonishing, truly desirable. It makes me want to stay, makes me almost forget home, makes me almost forget why I'm here and what I'm fighting for.

We go back to the elevator and head down to the commercial levels.

"Now," Felicity says as we walk. "Your parents know where to buy everything that they might need here in the city, so don't worry if you can't remember."

"Can't they just tell me then? What's the point of the tour?"

"Heavens, no! You need the proper training, lovey. I can't send you off only half introduced to your new home. If I did, I wouldn't be doing my job now, would I?"

I sigh. "I guess not."

"Cheer up, my darling. You'll be with your family soon enough."

Felicity steps out of the elevator and into a corridor with a jungle projection that leads to the main level, which houses the stores and restaurants.

The food store is about six times the size of the one back home. It reminds me of the first time I met Mace, and my heart aches to get back to him.

Felicity marches me up and down each street, pointing out building after building. It's incredible here. Back home, we only have the essentials. I peer into the large, squeaky-clean windows of the storefronts. The bakery window is lined with cakes and pastries, dusted in icing sugar and oozing with jelly. The clothing stores have mannequins in the windows in various poses.

I lose myself, staring at all the things they have here.

"Next level, dear. Chop, chop," Felicity says, snapping her fingers and heading back toward the elevator.

"What's on the next level?"

"Your new school. I'll quickly introduce you to your class."

My stomach lurches. *Oh God.*

Felicity leads me to the front desk inside the school. We sign our names on an electronic pad, indicating we are visitors. I'm so worked up that I almost forget to write Lilly's name.

"Now you remember your old teacher, Mr. Elvin, right?" *Oh no, no, no.* "You'll be in his classes again this year. You won't miss much, though we have made some changes to the subjects. Right this way, he's teaching now on the second floor."

I drag my feet. I don't know what to do. Mr. Elvin will see that I'm not Lilly. But will he say anything? We stop outside a classroom door and Felicity taps her knuckles against it three times.

I hear a woman's voice on the other side. "Come in."

My heart is in my mouth. Felicity pushes the door open and steps inside. I hide behind her. "I thought Mr. Elvin was teaching in this room?" I hear her say.

"Ah, yes. He starts next week once he and his family are settled," the woman says. I breathe again.

"I see. Well, that's a shame. It'd have been nice for Lilly to see her teacher." Felicity turns to the class. "Hello, class!" she says, offering no apology for disturbing their lesson. "I'd like to introduce you all to a new student who'll be starting next week. Class, this is Lilly Tanner." She reaches back and feels for my arm, pulling me farther into the classroom once she has hold of my sleeve.

Some students mumble their greetings. A few of the girls wave at me. I lift my hand up by my side and wave back. I scan the faces.

There.

Deep, green eyes stare back at me.

Finn.

I shake my head at him, slowly. Barely a movement, but I know he catches it because he looks away and back to his teacher.

"Well, I'll leave you all to your lessons," Felicity says. "Come along, Lilly."

I follow her out, daring one last look back at Finn. His eyes stay focused on the front of the classroom.

We reach the front desk and sign out again. "Now for some lunch," Felicity says. "Then, after that, we'll complete your orientation with a couple of forms that need to be filled out."

"I'm still a little full from breakfast," I say.

"Nonsense! You hardly touched your plate. You'll be hungry once you get there and smell the food. I guarantee it! Come along."

There's no arguing with this woman. I follow her back to the elevator and down to the cafeteria.

We cut to the front of the line again. Felicity unnecessarily flashes a badge at the checkout guy and orders ridiculously lavish pasta for her lunch.

"What would you like to try, sweetness?" she asks.

I shrug and look at the menu on the wall. There's too much to choose from. And even if I select an item by name, I then have to read through everything that's on it or comes with it. It's dizzying. In the end, I order what I think is a cheese and pickle sandwich, along with who knows what else. I'm not planning on eating it, anyway.

We take our seats and Felicity occupies herself by scrolling through her electronic notepad. I drum my fingers on the table.

Our meals arrive. Felicity switches the pad off and digs in. I just pick at mine, claiming that I don't feel too good. She tries to convince me to eat something, so I pick a little bread off and put it in my mouth, feeling uncomfortable with her watching me.

"We can't have you not eating, pumpkin," she says. "It's not healthy."

"I just don't feel well, that's all. I'll eat later once I'm settled."

Felicity rolls her eyes. "Well, all right. Just don't go passing out on me. It's not in my job description to deal with fainting teenagers." She pulls out a small compact mirror from her jacket pocket and checks her reflection, smoothing her hair down and discreetly picking her teeth.

"Oh my GOD!" she squeals, snapping the mirror shut. She whips around in her seat to face the cafeteria entrance. "Oh my God, oh my God, oh my God!" she sings, fanning her face.

"*What?*" I notice a crowd at the door, but I can't see what's happening.

"Wait right here," she says. "Don't move an inch until I get back. I'll only be a moment."

Felicity stands up straight and flattens out the creases in her skirt. "Oh, and clear the table and give it a wipe down. Quick as you can." She pushes her shoulders back and puffs out her chest, then disappears into the crowd.

I stand to follow her. But the entrance is blocked. I can't get out of the cafeteria. I'm reminded of the day of the riot in the sector and shiver.

I return to the table and clear it up, like Felicity asked. *It's okay,* I tell myself. *You only have a form to fill out and then you can go.* I'm so close to the end, to completing orientation, I just have to suffer through this last little bit. Lilly's call to report me will come this evening and it's only lunchtime. I'm almost certain the machines are on one of the first three floors, so how hard can it be to find them? I tell myself to be confident, to believe that I can do this and then go home.

Once the table is clear, I stand on my tiptoes and try to get a look at what all the commotion is about. I can see Felicity forcing her way through the bodies and back toward me. Hopefully that means we're leaving now. Then I see that there's a small group of people behind her. She's talking animatedly over her shoulder at them and then I catch sight of who is with her.

No—not *him*. Not Damien Hoist.

My heart sinks. She's bringing him over here—that's why she wanted me to clear up. A lump forms in my throat the size of an apple and impossible to swallow back down.

I sink into my seat and don't look up again. Then I feel their shadows fall over me.

"Lilly, dear," Felicity chirps. "Look who it is!"

I glance up. My stomach flips and cramps. Damien Hoist is looking right at me and I'm looking back at him. I smile—I have to—and it hurts my jaw. My teeth grind as I take in the rest of the group: two women and three men.

Seven sets of eyes are trained on me, crawling over my skin, my messy hair, my scruffy clothes. *You belong here,* I tell myself. *Act like you belong here.*

The women are dressed like Felicity. They both have dark hair, dragged back and flattened down into perfect buns. It looks painful. Their expressions are serious and both regard me with harsh eyes.

The men hold cruel expressions on their faces. One is younger than the other two. His hair is thick and swept back from his face with the help of a considerable amount of gel. Not a strand is out of place. The other two men are closer to my dad's age—perhaps a little older—and both have graying hair and neat moustaches that are trimmed in a straight line, sitting neatly above their top lips. They all wear smart suits, like Felicity's.

"Oh, isn't that sweet!" Felicity says. "She's gone all shy!"

My eyes snap to her. "I'm fine," I say, though my voice is shaky.

Damien reaches his hand out to me. I try not to flinch. He flashes his striking white teeth in a disturbing smile. "Nice to meet you," he says.

I'm sweating. I wipe a trembling palm on my jeans before reaching back to shake hands with the man I hate. "Nice to meet you, too," I lie.

"Sit down, sit down," Felicity insists. My stomach lurches again, a violent ache. I don't want them to join us—we were just about to leave. I hope they decline, hope that Damien has something better to do with his day.

Unfortunately not.

He allows Felicity to pull him down beside her and across from me. The youngest of the group sits next to me, while the other four take their seats at the nearest table to us.

141

"So, what brings you down here today, Damien?" Felicity asks. She says his name slowly and clutches onto his arm. Yuck. I cringe at how foolish she looks. I glance at the boy beside me and find he's smirking at them.

"I should show my face down here from time to time," Damien answers, flashing her that horrible smile. She melts and I look away. "Besides," he continues. "I get lonely in my office all day."

Felicity giggles and offers to visit him.

"I have a lot to do this afternoon," he answers. "So I'm afraid I can't stay long."

"I have to finish up orientation with little Lilly."

I look back up at the mention of my—*Lilly's*— name, just in time to see Damien lean over and whisper something in Felicity's ear, causing her to giggle some more. I turn my head to the side and notice that almost everyone in the room is watching us. No, not us. Damien.

"It's Lilly, right?" the boy beside me says.

I nod.

"I'm Cain, Damien's son."

I jerk back. His eyes meet mine. I stare at him, absorbed. He does have Damien's good looks, and his charm.

"Is something wrong?"

"No," I say. "Sorry. I just didn't realize there was another Hoist in the world."

He smiles. "My father keeps me away from the cameras. He's a tad overprotective. So, how are you finding the New World so far?"

"It's nice," I say lamely. "I'm ... looking forward to seeing more."

Cain smiles again. Across the table, Damien stands, ready to leave, which earns a pout from Felicity. His entourage, including his son, stands up as he does and groups together. Felicity reaches out for one last touch of Damien's hand.

"Sir, we really must go," one of the women insists.

"Yes. We have a lot to do this afternoon, sir," the other woman says in virtually the same tone. With my eyes closed I wouldn't be able to tell them apart.

In a tight cluster, they make their way out of the cafeteria and I let out a long breath. Felicity sighs deeply and cups her face in her hands.

"Shall we go?" I say, snapping her back from her thoughts, which I'm certain consist only of Damien.

"What? Oh, yes. Yes, dear. Let's get going."

We walk back through the forest corridor and I follow Felicity to another small square room like the screening room. I can't help but worry about Cain. Is he like his father? Will he inherit all of this someday?

"In here, darling," Felicity says, pulling me from my thoughts. She walks through an open doorway and the lights automatically turn on as we enter.

There are filing cabinets along the walls that reach right up to the ceiling. A large metal desk is at the front of the room, a white screen behind it. Several smaller desks are set out in rows like a school classroom. They all face the front of the room. It's cold in here, too.

"Take a seat at one of the desks, Lilly," Felicity instructs.

I do as she says and wait, biting my lower lip, while she opens drawers and collects all the forms she wants me to fill out.

"I know this is terribly old-fashioned," she says as she places the first form in front of me. "But we do like to have a hard copy of this as well as electronic."

I stare down at the form on the desk. I know most of the answers thanks to Lilly's quizzing. I start with her mother's name, her father's, her home address. Then it starts getting tricky and I sit staring blankly at questions I'm supposed to know the answers to. I skip a few and continue to write so Felicity doesn't notice that I'm stuck. I can stall as long as I want, but I'm never going to be able to fill this out completely.

Felicity's waist pings. The sound echoes around the small room and she sighs with irritation. "What now?" she mumbles.

Pulling a small device from her belt, she squints to read its screen. "For heaven's sake." She sighs again. "Lilly, dear, my services are required on the ground floor. Will you be all right for a short while if I leave you to continue filling out these forms?"

YES! "I'll be fine," I tell her, trying not to laugh. *This is perfect!*

"Excellent," she says. "When you're all done with those, I'll have your family come get you and take you home."

I smile at her. *That's fine. I'll be long gone by the time you get back.*

144

Felicity gathers her things and leaves the room. She closes the door behind her. Then I hear a click. *Oh, no.* Did she lock me in?

I spend a couple of excruciating seconds in my seat, giving Felicity time to get far enough away before I run over to the door and try the handle. I find that she did lock it, and I'm trapped. And when she comes back, she'll have Lilly's parents with her and they'll tell her I'm not Lilly. I don't even know what'll happen to me then.

I already know there aren't any air vents or windows I can climb through, but I'm desperate, so I look over the ceiling and wall anyway. Then I search for something sharp to use to pick the lock, even though I don't know how to pick any lock other than the one on my bedroom door. Still, I have to try *something*.

While searching the desk drawers, I hear movement on the other side of the door and my heart skips. Felicity is back already. It's over.

The handle rattles and shakes, and the lock twists and clicks. I make it across the room just in time to hide behind the door as it swings open. Someone steps inside. The footsteps are quiet, not like Felicity's loud heels. Still, I don't move, don't risk making even the smallest sound.

A boy's voice whispers my name.

The door is pulled back and I'm no longer hidden, I'm face-to-face with Finn.

"What are you doing here?" I say.

Finn has hair as black as mine that falls into his eyes. I remember Lilly telling me that Finn had a crush on me and suddenly feel embarrassed being so close to him.

"I should be asking you that, Sia. I heard Lilly Tanner was here, and instead *you* walked into my morning class."

"Right. Well, yeah. It's a long story," I say.

"You're pretending to be her?" He sighs.

"Yes. Please, Finn. Please don't tell them."

"I won't have to! They'll find out on their own. They aren't stupid, Sia. Look around you, look at what they've created, what they've done. What makes you think you can deceive them?"

"I'm desperate," I whisper. "Anyway, what do I have to lose? They've taken everything from me already."

Finn laughs, short and abrupt. "Believe me, they'll make you suffer if they find out. Don't think they won't because you've already suffered enough. Not to them you haven't—not if they figure out what you've done. And they will."

I gulp. "Why are you telling me this? Why are you even here?"

"I called Felicity away to buy us some time. I wanted to find out what you are up to."

"You called her away?"

"Yes. She won't be gone long, so we have to go now if you want to get out of here alive."

"No. I can't go. Not yet," I say.

Finn checks his watch. "Sia, I—"

146

"I need to find the cyborgs. Then I'll go," I say.

His eyes widen. "What for?"

"I can't tell you."

"You better, and quickly."

I shake my head.

"Who sent you?"

"No one. Finn, I can't tell you. I just need to find them. Then I'll leave the New World. I have a plan."

He sighs. "Come on."

"Where?"

"Out of here before Felicity comes back. We're not done talking." He grabs my arm and pulls. We go through a door, which opens onto a concrete staircase, and Finn leads me down.

"Where are you taking me?"

"To the machines," he says, and my heart rate quickens. I try to pull my wrist from his grasp but he's too strong. He stops outside a red door with the number 1 printed on it in yellow.

My eyes flick from Finn to the door. I take a deep breath and pull on the handle. The door opens a crack before Finn slams it shut. "God, Sia. What are you doing? You're going to get yourself killed."

"I told you—"

"I know. You 'can't tell me'," he says, making air quotes with his fingers. "Well, how's this? I'm not letting you go until you do." He holds my wrist. I struggle but can't break free. "Sia, please stop. I'd never hurt you—"

"You're hurting me now!"

He pulls back, only slightly. "I'm not trying to. I just need you to start talking."

"I can't! And I don't have much time left. You *have* to let me go. Please!"

"Just tell me who sent you."

"Nobody! Nobody knows I'm here."

"Then why did you come?" he asks. I squeeze my eyes shut. "You can trust me. I want to help you."

"I want to see the machines."

"You already said that. What do you want to see them for?"

"Because . . . Because I'm going to fight them when they come to the sector," I blurt out.

"I *knew* it. You're not fighting them on your own, though, are you?" I shake my head. He leans closer. "You're not the only group of rebels, Sia," he whispers in my ear.

I gasp. "You?"

"I'm on your side. I was in your group before I was brought here. I haven't managed to get in contact with the sector yet, though. I was supposed to tell them about the machines."

"You've seen them?" I ask, realizing that Finn is our informer. But why did he never get in contact with us?

"Yes. I can tell you all about them on the way out." He moves back and takes my hand, guiding me back up the staircase, but I hold my ground.

"I don't want you to tell me about them. I want to see for myself."

Finn drops his head and releases my hand. He rubs his face. "They'll be looking for you."

"Then we better hurry," I say.

Finn hesitates, running his hands through his hair.

"Finn, come on. This is why I came here. Just let me see them, then I can go back and inform everyone what we are up against."

"If I promise to show you, you have to do everything I say. And I mean *everything*. You can't speak to anyone, you have to stay out of sight as much as possible, and you can never leave my side unless I say otherwise. Understood?"

I nod once, sharply. Finn takes a deep breath and pushes the red door open.

To my relief, the corridor we find ourselves on is empty. It displays a projection of space. The lighting is purple and tiny stars make up galaxies with planets that litter the surface of the tiles. I touch Earth and it spins.

"Someone's coming," Finn warns.

A man and woman, both holding electronic pads like Felicity's, come around the corner. They stop talking when they see us. "What are you kids doing down here?" the man says.

"Science project," Finn replies, quickly and calmly.

"Who's supervising you?" the woman asks.

"We're on the way to meet them now," Finn replies.

We continue down the corridor and Finn stops outside a door. "You'll have to go in there and get a lab coat."

"What? Why me?"

"Because someone might recognize me. If you want to do this, you're going to have to go in there on your own."

I close my eyes. *I can do this. I got here on my own. I'm brave. I can do this.* I repeat those words in my head as I step into the staff room alone.

It's very basic. There are a few tables and chairs shoved up against the wall to my right, and a row of kitchen counters lining the back wall. In the corner are four ratty sofas that look like they've been rescued from one of the old dumps. On a rack to my left, beside the door, are white lab coats. I pull two down and ball them up, shoving them under my arm and turning to leave.

"Hey!"

I freeze.

"What are you doing in here? Are you lost? You're not meant to be in here."

I turn back to see a bald, skinny man with glasses looking back at me. I choke on my words. "Um . . . l-looking for my father."

"Who's your father?"

"Coat," I add quickly.

"Excuse me?" the man says, putting his hands on his hips.

"I said 'coat'. I was looking for my father's coat, but I have it now." He narrows his eyes. "He's speaking to a colleague and asked me to run back and get it for him."

"And what exactly were you doing down here in the first place?"

"Science project," I say.

He considers me. "All right. Well, go on, then. Before you get yourself into trouble."

Finn is leaning against the wall, waiting for me outside the door. "How'd it go?" he asks. I hand him one of the lab coats. "What's this? I told you I wasn't coming in with you."

"What? I thought you meant in the staff room."

Finn shakes his head. "The lab too. Only staff are allowed in there. Science project or not, we wouldn't be admitted into that room. It's too risky for me. You'll be fine—no one knows you."

"Finn, I don't know. I'm not sure I'm ready for this."

"You better be. You came all this way. I'll take you to the lab, then I'll wait for you in the stairwell. You come there when you're done, okay?"

I chew my lip. "Okay."

Finn leaves me outside a glass door and tells me what to do once I'm inside. I can see the lab through the glass but the door requires a key code to open. I let my hair down, so it falls around my face, keeping me somewhat hidden.

Someone's coming toward the door from inside the lab. I back up so they can't see me. The door opens and I start walking through it. I squeeze between the person and the frame, mumbling my thanks. And I'm in.

I weave my way between cluttered desks and workers in white coats. Everything is charts and graphs and figures. I follow Finn's instructions. He's been in here once before—when he first came to the New World.

I find a small separate room, deep in the lab, where the cyborgs are tested. Right where Finn said it would be. The door is locked: Restricted Access printed in bold type and underlined on the door. There's a small window at the top of the door, so I push up onto my tiptoes to peek through it.

My head feels like it's going to explode.

I grip the door to stop myself from staggering back and crying out in terror. The machines are tall, *so tall*. Their silver, skeletal bodies are wired up to rows and rows of power sockets. Thick tubes stretch from the backs of their heads and spines. Their eyes are black holes in a metal skull. Their fingers stretch to a length three times longer than mine and come to sharp points like knives. I can already feel the agony of them ripping into my skin, tearing out my heart, ending my life.

"Amazing, aren't they?"

I whip around, eyes wide, only to come face-to-face with the kid from the cafeteria—Cain. My ears are ringing, I feel like I'm going to collapse. He steadies me. Does he recognize me? I try to keep my face hidden behind my hair, but I worry that it's too late to hide now.

I force myself to speak. "Sure are."

"I like to come down here and see them from time to time. They're beyond fascinating. Technology at its best. Wouldn't you agree?" Cain taps on the door and waits for it to open. "Lilly," he adds, and my heart skips. "You shouldn't be down here." He smirks. Then the door opens and he steps inside without another word.

I want to run, but I'm rooted to the ground. Why didn't he do anything? I press my body against the door and look into the room again. They're running tests. One of the machines is now unhooked and in the middle of the room. The workers stand behind a barrier, the bottom half concrete, the top half glass. I watch them use a handheld device to turn the cyborg on. The machine heads straight for them and crashes into the barrier. It keeps walking, even though there's nowhere to go. It smacks against the window over and over and over. No matter how hard it hits, the glass does not shatter. Not even a chip.

It stops.

Turns.

Comes for me.

It's on the other side of the door in a second, smashing against the glass window on the door. I shriek and fall backward. Some of the workers in the lab behind me stop what they're doing and come over to help me up. A woman pushes my hair out of my face. "Are you all right?" she asks.

"I think so," I say.

She helps me to my feet. "What did you expect, standing so close?"

"What do you mean?"

She purses her lips. "Oh, you're new. They're drawn to human life. It was bound to sense you, standing too close to the door. Don't worry, we've all done it. Spooky, aren't they?" I swallow, and try to remember how to breathe. *They're drawn to human life.* Hiding from them really is no good. Suddenly I'm glad Lilly's coming here, rather than

153

sitting on top of that hill thinking the machines will pass through the sector and leave her alive up there.

"Are you sure you're okay?" the woman says, still holding my shoulders. She guides me to a desk and sits me down on a chair.

"Huh? Yeah, I'm fine."

"Can I get you a glass of water?"

Before I can answer, a loud banging sound shakes the lab. Four fists slam into the glass doors. They rattle like they're going to shatter. I duck down and hide under the desk. But before long, four hands reach under, grab my arms, and drag me out. I struggle and kick at the two men, but it's no use. They're huge—muscle and power. They rip off the lab coat I'm wearing, leaving it in a torn heap on the floor.

"What is going on?" the woman shrieks.

"It doesn't concern you, miss," one of the guards says, clamping down harder on my arm. My pulse throbs and my arm starts to go numb.

Once I stop fighting back, the two men walk me out of the lab and into the space corridor. They both keep a hand on my shoulders. I'm guided to the glass elevator and up to Level 3.

Felicity is waiting for me in the room where she'd left me. She's at the desk, tapping her long, black-painted fingernails on the metal surface. She looks furious. "How on *earth* did you get out of here?" she chides when I'm escorted in.

I look her in the eye. "Through the door."

"I locked it. I know I locked it."

"If you had, I wouldn't have gotten out."

Felicity stands up and takes a step toward me. "I don't know how you did it, but you're making me look very bad here. Now tell me the truth, or you will be punished. Do you understand?"

In the corner of the room, someone clears her throat. The sound makes me jump and I spin around. There's a family of four sitting at the desks in the back corner of the room. A woman, a man, and two young blonde girls—Lilly's family. I recognize her parents.

Lilly's mother clasps her hands together and holds them up to her chest. Her eyes are wet. "That's not Lilly," she says. Her voice shakes. I fear the three words she just spoke will cost me my life.

"Excuse me?" Felicity says.

Lilly's mom shakes her head. Her face is red, swollen with emotion. She hugs her chest and looks away. Lilly's dad, Mr. Tanner, puts a hand on his wife's shoulder. The two girls cling to their mother's dress. "She said that this girl is not Lilly," Mr. Tanner says. "She is not our daughter."

"That's impossible! She provided us with her prints and they matched Lilly's."

Mr. Tanner's eyes widen, his gaze flicks to me. "What did you do to our daughter? How did you get the electronic pad? How did you get her fingerprints?"

I don't respond. What's the point now? It's over. Felicity calls the guards back and they bind my hands behind my back. The cold metal pinches my skin, clamped too tight. The metallic smell mixed with my fear makes me feel like I'm going to be sick. *They caught you*, I keep replaying in my head, like it's not real. *They caught you.*

Felicity and the two guards lead me out of the room and into the stairwell that Finn took me through earlier. *Finn.* I wonder if he's still waiting for me down there. We walk down the stairs, pass the red door with the yellow number 2, the red door with the yellow number 1. Finn isn't here. I let out a sigh of relief.

We go down another level, underground. The door here is black and instead of a number it reads NO ADMITTANCE. The metal chain rattles between my trembling hands. They lead me through a series of corridors as dull and gloomy as the first one. There are no projections down here, only gray concrete and lights that flicker and buzz.

At the very end of the corridor is a huge metal door. One guard wrenches it open and the other shoves me inside. There's a single table positioned in the center with a chair on either side. Each leg of furniture is drilled into the floor with thick screws. They sit me in one of the chairs and tie my already bound hands to its back. A bright bulb overhead spotlights me. The guards stand behind me, one in each corner. The silence is thick and heavy, but my heart pounds so loud in my ears that they must be able to hear it. I blink sweat from my eyes. I don't want them to know how afraid I am.

Moments later, Felicity enters, followed by two other guards, who take their positions in the remaining two corners of the room. Felicity sits on the metal chair across from me and rests her elbows on the table.

"I don't usually take care of this side of things," Felicity says. "But under the circumstances, I'm too interested in you to hand the case over to somebody else. You've played *me* for a fool." She stabs her finger into her chest. "And you will answer for it. Is that clear, my love?"

I stare at the table, ignoring her. One of the guards behind me steps forward. I feel him come closer, then he hits the back of my head. He shoves me so hard that my head falls, smacking against the table. Blood explodes from my nose. The pain isn't instant, but it flares up quickly, throbbing intensely.

"Do you *know* what you've done? You stupid, stupid girl. Do you think your friend Lilly and her family won't pay for their part in this, too?"

My head snaps up. I'm seeing spots, and blood is running into my mouth and coating my teeth with its coppery taste. "They had no part in this," I say.

"Then tell me exactly what happened."

"I want to live here," I lie.

"And you thought it would be that simple? You thought that you could just walk in here under a false name and never be discovered?"

"No. But I was desperate," I say.

"Right you were. So, I'll ask you again: How did you manage all of this?"

I don't answer. I don't know how to answer. I need time to think.

"Maybe you need a little push," Felicity says, rising to her feet. The four guards follow her out of the room, their heavy boots pounding the floor in rhythm. I'm left alone.

I use the time to think. When they return I'll tell them that I attacked Lilly and took the electronic pad from her. That I forced her to help me.

The door opens and Lilly's dad steps inside.

"Mr. Tanner," I say. "What are you—?"

He's shaking. Behind him, the guards carry a cyborg into the room. As soon as I see it I start pulling at my bonds, struggling in my seat, trying to get free. Not this, anything but this. Why are they bringing that monster in here?

I can't breathe. I can't breathe.

They attach the cyborg to the wall at its waist with heavy metal chains. They do the same to Mr. Tanner. Monster and man are side by side.

"What are you doing?" I ask, voice trembling.

No one answers me. Mr. Tanner trembles and begs the guards to let him go. They ignore him, too. I push against my chair, try to rip it from the floor. I can't get up, I can't get free, it's hopeless.

"Stop!" I cry out.

A speaker crackles to life. Felicity's voice echoes around the room. "You should have answered my questions, pumpkin. You only have yourself to blame for this."

"I'll answer them!" I shout. "Just stop this. Let him go!"

The speaker static cuts off, and the machine moves its head.

"No!" I scream. "Felicity, please! I'll talk, just turn it off."

Mr. Tanner moves as far away from the machine as his chains will allow, but he can't get beyond a foot. The guards made sure of that. Too easily, the cyborg grips Mr. Tanner's arm and pulls him back. The frightened man starts to yell as the machine crushes every bone in his hand. Blood runs down his arm, where the cyborg's long fingers have ripped into his skin, and drips onto the floor. An awful crunching noise tears through the room as the cyborg rips Mr. Tanner's hand right off. The machine drops the hand to the floor where it lands with a sickening squelch. Then I start to scream, *really* scream.

The machine pulls Mr. Tanner to it and crushes him to death. Once he's dead, the machine releases him and stills, and the door creaks open again.

My face is wet. I can't use my hands to wipe the tears from my cheeks and the salty wetness mixes with the metallic taste in my mouth. The guards take Mr. Tanner's body and the cyborg away, but the smell of blood and images of mutilation stay with me. Felicity takes her place across from me again. I can't look at her.

"Now, tell me how you got here. Tell me what plan you and Lilly cooked up. I want to hear it. And if you don't, if you miss one tiny detail, I'll bring one of the little girls in next."

I swallow. "You'll leave her family alone if I tell you what happened?"

"Yes, dear. I'll leave her family unharmed."

"I used the electronic pad at Lilly's house to call. You know I did, you answered," I say, still not meeting her eyes.

"So Lilly led you to it?"

"Against her will."

"I very much doubt that," Felicity says.

I look up at her. She's smiling. "Why are you asking me these questions when you already know the answers?"

"Very clever," she says, sliding an electronic pad toward me. The screen plays footage of Lilly and me going to the Tanners' house. "It doesn't look to me like she's being forced. It looks as if she's trying to hide herself from the cameras as she leads you to her house, don't you think?"

She's got me and she knows it.

Felicity laughs. "Tell me, what happened when you got inside the house? Did she hand you the leaflet and listen to your call?"

I nod, defeated.

"Ha! Then what? Lilly pressed her thumb on the pad when asked to provide confirmation of identity, then you got on the aircraft in her place? Genius! I reward you girls for your efforts, I really do. And one last thing—your name."

I scowl.

"*Your name*," Felicity insists.

"Sia."

"Sia . . .?"

"Morgan," I say. "Sia Morgan."

"Very good." Felicity waves the guards forward. "Take Sia to the cells while we figure out what to do with her, and do it quietly. I don't want this getting out."

The guards untie me and push me off the chair. Once I regain my balance, they march me out of the room with Felicity leading the way. "And send someone to her sector to visit Lilly," she says.

"What?" I snap. "You said if I cooperated you'd leave her family alive."

"Her family, yes. But Lilly played a crucial part in this little scheme and must face the consequences of her actions."

"It was me! She only did it because I made her—"

"Enough! I'll be seeing you in a short while, dear."

The guards shove me back along the corridors and outside to a small, ugly building. Inside, the smell hits me first—bitter and sour. I try to breathe through my mouth. It's not much better—I can almost taste the air as it hits the back of my throat. It's a small jail with nothing inside—there aren't even lights. It's dark and damp and cold. The barred cell doors are all open—no one else is in here. The guards lead me to the farthest cell from the door. The smell gets worse the deeper into the building we go. My hands are untied and I'm heaved inside. Then the door is slammed shut and locked.

Once I'm left alone, I rattle on the bars, try to squeeze through them, *anything*. I pace the cell. I can't stop moving. I need to get out. I try everything I can think of and nothing pays off. There's nothing to do but wait.

I want to cry, but I don't.

I want to scream, but I don't.

I sit, quietly, and await my sentence with no idea what they'll do to me.

6 DAYS

I shouldn't have fallen asleep.

I don't know how I did. I don't know how I closed my eyes. I don't know how I could relax for even a second in this awful place.

Outside the cell door is the sound of jangling keys and groaning metal. They're here for me. It's time. I hear the door open, but I can't see a thing. I can only just make out my own pale hands in front of me. There are no windows in this cell. No moonlight shining through bars to give me even a clue of what time it is or who's standing in the cell with me.

"Who's—?" I begin.

"Shh."

I tense. I'm scared, *so scared*. I sit up straight, listen. Thousands of scenarios flash through my mind: I'll be publicly executed, or the guards will shoot me here, or they'll do to me what they did to Mr. Tanner with the cyborg, or they'll leave me here and let me rot and waste away until I'm nothing but a pile of bones.

Hard, calloused hands rest on top of mine. I jump at the sudden contact. "Shh," the voice says again. Lips touch

163

my hair. Warm breath weaves through each strand. "It's me,
Finn. You're okay. I'm here for you," he whispers.

He laces his fingers through mine. "Sia, say something."
I can't.

"Did they hurt you?" Finn runs his free hand up my
arm, slowly, carefully, until it finds my neck, my ears, my
face. He touches my cheek, wipes away the wetness from
my tears with his fingertips. "Sia," he breathes. "Sia, it's all
right." He guides my head to his shoulder and strokes my
hair.

I choke. "Finn?"

His face is pressed against mine and I feel him smile.
"It's me, I'm here," he soothes.

I hug him harder. "I thought they'd come to kill me."

He eases me back, feels for my face in the dark again,
and brushes tangled hair out of my eyes. His touch is so
gentle, so careful. "Would you like to go home instead?"
he whispers. His face is closer than I thought. I nod, and
my forehead rubs against his. His breath catches and there's
no sound at all in the cell. No noise at all around us. Until
sharp stilettos crack the silence. The unmistakable sound of
pointy heels clicking on concrete.

Finn hoists us both up and guides us out of the cell.
He navigates to the front of the building and into the first
cell by a side entrance. He pushes me up against the wall,
in the corner beside the metal door, and presses his body
into mine. Finn's breath tickles my neck, shallow and fast.

Felicity steps into the jail and Finn stops breathing alto-
gether. The dull footsteps of guards follow her. I'm stiff,

rigid, my limbs tense up tight against Finn's body. Then he pulls away. Cold air slaps me. Without him I'm vulnerable, exposed.

He holds my hand and crouches low, pulling me down into the same position as him. His footsteps are careful, cautious, silent.

Felicity and her guards are at the back of the building now. I see the bright yellow beam of a flashlight bobbing around as they approach what was my cell. She says my name and I freeze. "The decision has been made as to what to do with you," she continues.

I want to hear more.

Felicity's footsteps stop. There is a moment of silence, then she shrieks. Finn tugs at my arm and we slip out through the open door. We straighten up but don't let go of each other.

And then we're running.

"That . . . complicates things," Finn pants. We're heading back to the New World, the last place on earth I want to be. Finn seems to sense my hesitation. "It's the only way," he says.

There's someone waiting for us, a silhouetted figure propping open a door.

"Who's that?" I say, panicking and pulling Finn back.

"It's all right, come on." He urges me forward, quicker now.

A split second later, there's shouting behind us. Felicity is screaming across the grounds to us—to me. "We'll catch you, you stupid girl! You *will* die! Painfully and slowly!"

My body is ice.

"Don't listen to her," Finn says. "Block her out, we're almost there."

"Shoot her," Felicity orders.

I stiffen, brace myself. Then I'm dragged through the door into the New World. I hadn't even realized we were so close. Bullets hit the metal door. The sound is deafening.

"Oh, God," I sigh, falling to my knees.

"No time," Finn says, yanking me back up to my feet and hauling me up the stairs. His fingers dig into me. He's being rough with me. *He's trying to get me out of here alive.*

Alarms scream to life.

My legs are on fire. Still, I force them to keep pushing, keep moving, keep running. Finn is in front of me and now there's another boy behind me. The three of us dash up the concrete stairs. Hundreds of steps. My feet slap against them, harder and harder, climbing higher and higher. I'm dizzy with the motion and the noise and the fear. My throat burns. Each breath I take is agony. My legs feel like they're about to snap in half. The sirens ring in my head, pounding against my skull, vibrating every part of my body. Voices a couple of levels below us are loud and angry and bloodthirsty.

They want me.

The boys keep running, never waver, never stop. I feel like I'm trapped in a dream, running and never getting anywhere. Nothing but concrete steps surround me: they're beneath me, in front of me, behind me. I'm running but nothing seems to change.

Then I remember the doors. The red doors with the yellow numbers—they're changing. I focus on them. The numbers are increasing, indicating that I'm getting somewhere, that I'm actually moving forward.

19

32

57

Finn crashes into door 60. Cold air slams into me, almost knocking me back down the stairs. The boy behind steadies me.

I run out into the night sky. I skid on the gravel outside. We're so high. Down below, the Rough is in total darkness. The city's surrounded by a soft blue glow from the laser gates.

"This way," Finn calls. He's running across the asphalt toward a dark bulky shape I recognize as a New World aircraft. *I'm going home.*

I run, despite my screaming muscles. I don't look back until I'm on the aircraft. Finn hits the side twice, a signal to the pilot.

"Wait! What about you?" I scream over the noise.

"I have to stay here," Finn says. "There's still work to be done."

"But you helped me escape. What'll happen to you?"

Finn shrugs. "Just worry about yourself and saving your sector."

"But what if I can't save them? You should come, you can—"

Finn holds my face in between his hands. "You're amazing, Sia," he says. "Start believing it."

The other boy pulls Finn back as the aircraft's rotor blades pick up speed. *Believe it*, Finn mouths, then the door slides closed and I climb into the sky.

On the journey back to the sector I think about Finn and the rebels in the New World. There are people inside trying to bring it down, and they're good at what they do. I think about the last thing Finn said to me, and I think about how much I've done and how much is yet to be done. I am a rebel now. I can fight against the New World, but it only means something if I believe I can succeed. *Believe it.*

We land in the sector and the pilot opens the doors for me.

"Where will you go?" I ask.

He squints up at the sky, the sun's rising behind the wall. "Into the Rough," he says. "I can't go back to the New World, they'll be waiting for me."

I gasp. "The *Rough*? How will you survive out there? Haven't you heard the stories?"

The pilot laughs, deep and hearty. "I think I'll manage."

"Have you been there before?" He nods. I almost ask him to take me with him, to wait here while I go get Dad and Mace and the rest of the group, but I don't. To abandon the rest of the sector's citizens would be selfish.

He leaves me standing in the sector, watching the aircraft rise back up into the sky and over the wall. I turn to see the shutters of the houses opening up for the end of curfew. My heart leaps into my throat when I see the number 6 displayed on the clock tower. It was 8 the last time I saw it.

Once I have my bearings, I turn to head home. There's so much to tell Dad and Mace, so much to do in preparation for the arrival of the machines. I sprint down an empty street, listening to the groan of the shutters opening on each house I pass.

Lilly.

I skid in the road. *Lilly.* I scream her name.

I take a sharp turn leading me to the Tanners' house and run so fast I almost fall over. When I reach her house, the front door is closed. I push it open. The rooms are still and dark. I step into the hall and call out for her. There's no answer, no sound.

The door to the living room is open a crack. I shove it and see Lilly's foot sticking out from behind the sofa, but the rest of her body is hidden by the furniture.

I take another step. I can see her legs now—jeans ripped at the knees, patches of mud on the skin underneath—one is straight, the other bent.

I hold my breath and edge farther into the room. I'm trembling, shaking so fiercely I'm surprised I'm still standing. She isn't moving. I see her body now, only her face is still hidden from me, and I'm not sure I want to see it. I look for the rise and fall of her chest, the slight sound of her breath, a twitch, a movement, *anything*.

Taking a final, unsteady step her face comes into view. It sends me to my knees. Her blue eyes are wide, frozen in shock. Her cheeks are sticky with dry tears. And there's a single bullet hole in her forehead.

I scream.

I scream until my lungs feel like they're going to burst.

I scream until my throat feels like it's been ripped out and stuffed back in again.

I did this. I caused this. This is my fault. I hold her hand. "I'm so sorry, Lilly," I whisper. My tears run fast. "I'm *so sorry* that I did this to you."

I sit with Lilly for a long time. It's torture when I leave her. I close her eyes, but it doesn't feel like enough.

I sit outside her front door, wondering what to do next. I know I have to go home. I've been away for almost two days and I'm sure Dad and Mace are worried. Turning back toward Lilly's house one last time, I lift my gaze and touch my palm to the front door. "I'm sorry," I whisper again. Then I step away.

Outside my house, I flatten my hair down and wipe the remaining tears from my cheeks, then I ease open the front door and step inside.

Dad's in front of me in an instant. "Sia." He grabs my face between his hands and looks at me closely. His eyes shine. "You're home. Oh, thank God, you're home." He hugs me tight. "Your face. What happened to your face?"

"I'm sorry, Dad," I breathe.

"Where have you been?" he asks, his words muffled against my hair. "I've been so worried about you. Why would you lie about needing to rest and then disappear like that?"

I shake my head.

"I went into your room and you were gone. I searched the entire sector for you, we all have. You don't know how much training time we've spent looking for you."

I put my hands out. *Stop*, please. Guilt stabs me hard. "I'll explain," I say. "I'll tell you, I just . . . I'm sorry."

Dad walks me to the kitchen, his hand on my elbow, guiding me. I glance in the hall mirror as we walk past it. My eyes and nose are swollen. Dried blood sticks to my lips and chin.

Dad pulls out a chair and I drop into it. He wets a cloth in the sink and wipes the blood from my face. Cold drops of water land on my lap. He throws the cloth in the trashcan once he's done.

The chair opposite screeches against the floor when he pulls it out for himself, then groans as he eases his weight into it.

He watches me, waits. I can't find the words. I've practiced what to say, what to tell him, but now I don't know how. Not after learning how worried he's been, the search parties he's sent out for me, the training time everyone's wasted.

"I'm sorry," I whisper again. I feel like I can't apologize enough.

"You're safe now, that's all that matters. You have to understand how scared I've been for you."

"I do understand. I'm—"

"Sorry. I know. Tell me where you were all this time."

"I made a new friend. Lil—" My voice catches on her name. I squeeze my eyes shut and will the image of her dead body away.

"Sia?"

"My friend, her name is—*was*—Lilly."

"Was?"

"She's dead now. Because of me."

"You're not making any sense. Have you hurt someone, is that why you ran away?"

"I didn't . . . I didn't run away. I didn't intentionally hurt Lilly, either." I growl and slam my hand down on the table. "I'm saying this all *wrong*."

Dad holds my hands but I pull them away. I don't want him to touch me, not after what I've done. Not before he knows.

"Lilly's family was chosen to go to the New World, but Lilly stayed behind. She didn't want to go there. I met her, up on the hill. She was hiding, waiting for the cyborgs to destroy the sector and move on. After the first training session, I felt . . . I felt *good*. I felt confident and thought maybe we'd actually stand a chance of surviving this. But when I came home I started to really think about it and doubt crept in. It's not that I doubt our abilities—I know we're good fighters—but I panicked because we're preparing to fight something we know nothing about."

"My source in the New World—"

"Is never going to get back to you," I say, cutting him off. "I think you already know that. It's been too long."

Dad rubs his hands over his face. "It's hard, Sia. Trying to run a group and keep everyone's spirits up, giving them hope. Six sectors have fallen. There have been no survivors. I pinned everything on my contact's information and it never came. Now there's nothing to do but keep training as we have been and hope that it's enough."

"It will never be enough," I tell him, remembering the monstrous machines in the lab. The cyborgs we've all been dreading are nowhere near as bad as what's really coming. I know because they're not scared enough. I fell apart when I saw it, and I know others will, too.

"I won't have you destroy the hope I've worked so hard to build. I won't let you take that from them," Dad protests.

"I've seen them," I say, so quietly that he doesn't hear me at first. I speak again, louder. "I've seen the machines."

Dad opens his mouth, then closes it again. "Wh—? How?" he stutters, shaking his head.

"I-I went to the New World."

"That's not possible," he breathes.

"I used L-Lilly's identity," I'm shaking but continue. "I saw them."

Dad gets up and leaves the room. When he returns he has a sheet of paper and a pencil with him. He puts them on the table in front of me. "Draw," he says.

"What? I-I can't." My hands are shaking too much. My mind isn't clear.

"DRAW!" he demands. "You went there, to that . . . that place, risked your life, and didn't breathe a word of it

to me. I have wasted so much time—their precious time—
to find you. I have forfeited training sessions for you. And
all along you were . . . you were . . ." He slams his fist on
the table, then pushes the paper closer to me. "Just draw
the machine. Let's hope your stupidity pays off in some
way with this."

"Dad, I—"

"I don't want to hear any more. I can't, not right now.
I'm going to go call off the search and let people know
you're back."

"Mace, is he—?"

"He hasn't stopped looking for you since we realized
you were gone."

The guilt I felt earlier cuts deeper.

"I'm sorry," I say again, but they're empty words.

Dad turns away from me. "Just draw the machine while
I'm gone." The front door slams shut, leaving me alone in
the house.

I pick up the pencil.

In front of me, I have several sketches of the machines
surrounded by notes of what little I learned about them.
They're drawn to human life echoes in my head. I drop the
pencil and flex my hand.

Upstairs, I take a shower. The hot water helps to relieve
my tight, aching limbs. I've only been standing beneath the
spray a couple of minutes when the water suddenly runs
cold. Then it cuts out completely. I turn it off, then back
on again. Nothing.

I step out and dry off. Looking in the mirror, I find my pale skin is covered in bruises, including my face. I slip into a clean pair of dark jeans and a tight long-sleeved black top with a loose T-shirt pulled on over it. Then I brush the knots out of my wet hair and tie it into a bun.

In the bathroom, I try the light switch. On, off, on, off. Nothing. Then I try my bedroom light and that doesn't work, either.

Something's wrong.

Is it just our house or all of them? Was it stupid to come back here? They'll have seen me on the cameras, they'll know I escaped and came back.

I take the stairs two at a time and close all the blackout shutters. Dad returns while I'm working at sealing them shut. "What are you doing?" he says, as I slam the hallway shutters closed. He's with two other men and Mace.

Mace. I want more than anything to be in his arms, but I can't stop, not even for a second. They're coming.

They're coming.

"Sia, stop!" Dad yells, but I can't. They're coming.

"Help me!" I say. "Close them all!"

One of the men doesn't look much older than me. His hair is shaved short and he has piercings all over his ears: the tragus, the lobe, the rim. He's wearing a vest, and every visible bit of skin on his chest and arms is covered with tattoos. Suddenly I remember him from training. I remember thinking: *he looks like a soldier.* But I can't remember his name. He helps me close the shutters.

The other man stays beside Dad. I see it's Miles; I know him. He's Dad's best friend. His hair is completely gray. I wouldn't say Miles was strong, but he's not weak, either, and he seems as determined as my dad that we're going to win this fight.

Mace is still standing in the open doorway, just behind Dad and Miles.

"Get inside, now!" I yell.

As soon as Mace steps inside the foyer I slap both my hands against the door and slam it shut, turning the locks. Then I hear it. The sound I've been waiting for. Distant, but there.

They're here.

Mace turns to me, raising his eyes to meet mine. "Is it true? You really went there?" he asks.

"We can't talk about it now. They're almost here."

"Who is? You're not making any sense, Sia. What's gotten into you?"

"They're coming! Can't you hear that?" I point up. Mace frowns and listens, then his face twists.

The aircraft's louder now. I pull open one of the shutters and peer out of the crack. I can see the aircraft—a black dot in the sky heading straight for us. I shouldn't have come back here.

Mace, Dad, and the other two men are on alert now. I look around and spot the kitchen window. "This way," I say, leading them into the kitchen.

Dad packs up the cyborg sketches. On the kitchen table is the red box he used to take to work with him, and he's laid out some tools beside it. I take the hammer and hook it through one of the belt loops on my jeans. Then we're out the window and running through the tight gap behind our row of houses.

There are no cameras back here. It's a tiny space between two rows of houses, so small that we have to shuffle sideways through it, so tight that the walls scratch my shoulders through my clothes.

The aircraft is so close now I can feel it. The wind picks up around us, howls as it rips through the alley. Dad stops before he reaches the end of the row. He holds up his palm. "They'll see us on the cameras," he says, jerking his head toward the street.

New plan. We work our way back along the houses, knocking on kitchen windows until someone answers our calls. An old woman slides hers open. She knows my dad. He's speaking to her, but I can't hear what they're saying. Then she steps back and Dad motions for us to follow him into her house.

We sit at the kitchen table, which is covered with a cream lace cloth, on cushioned chairs. The woman closes the shutters over the windows. Then she leaves the room, shutting us inside. I can hear the Reports in the next room.

"What's happening?" I whisper.

"We can stay in here for a little while, while we figure out what to do," Dad says. "What happened in the New World, Sia? Why have they come here for you?"

"Once they found out I wasn't Lilly, they planned on killing me. But a guy from school—Finn—saved me. He got me out of there and back home. If it weren't for him I—"

I'd be dead.

"Earlier, the water and power shut off and that only happens when the house isn't in use anymore. They're here to kill me, Dad."

I don't know how long it has been before the old woman—her name is Ree—comes back into the kitchen to tell us our house is on fire.

Dad rushes to the front window and I follow him. He opens it and we watch black smoke billow into the sky as the hungry flames claim our home. The fire roars in victory. I can taste the destruction on my tongue, the acrid smoke filling my throat and burning. I'm supposed to be in there. What happens when they find out I'm not?

I'm dead anyway. Six days.

Ree won't let us stay. Right now, the street is crowded, which provides us some cover from the cameras, but it won't be for long. People from the houses closest to ours have evacuated. They're standing in the street, watching our house burn and hoping it doesn't spread to theirs. I hope it doesn't, too.

One in our group, Remy, goes home, and the rest of us head for Miles's house. It's the nearest to ours—just a couple of streets away. Miles lives alone, so there's plenty of room for us. In our attempt to avoid the cameras, it takes much longer to get there than it should.

It's late afternoon and Miles gives Dad the sofa to sleep on. He shows me to the spare room where I'll stay, then leaves me to settle in. I sit on the twin bed and lean against the wall. I can smell smoke in my hair, on my clothes, coating my skin. And this is all I have left—the clothes I'm wearing, and the hammer hooked to my jeans.

There's a tap at the door.

"Come in," I say.

Mace hovers near the open door. "Hey," he says.

"Hey."

He closes the door and sits beside me on the bed. Our thighs touch. He smells of smoke, too. Mace tucks a small piece of loose hair behind my ear. "I was so worried about you these past two days," he whispers. "I can't believe you were in the New World the whole time. I looked everywhere for you and I couldn't find you. But you weren't even in the sector. You were somewhere I couldn't get to you and that . . . that kills me. If anything had happened to you there, I wouldn't have been able to protect you from it. I wouldn't have even known."

"Mace, the whole point of joining Dad's group is so that I can defend myself. I don't need someone to protect me." I feel bad as soon as the words leave my mouth, but I want him to fight *with* me, not *for* me.

He initially looks hurt, but quickly recovers. "I understand. Just say you won't do anything like that again. Promise me that you won't."

"I promise," I say.

Mace cups my face with his hand. His gaze flicks from my eyes to my lips and he guides my face toward his. I close my eyes as his lips touch mine and the world disappears.

His hands move around my waist and I lean into him. My skin tingles under the pressure of his touch. Slowly, I reach out for him, heart hammering, and run my hands around his neck, burying the tips of my fingers into his messy hair.

Too soon, he breaks the kiss and rests his forehead against mine. His eyes are closed. "I wish I'd done that sooner," he whispers, then leans forward and rests his lips against my ear. It makes me dizzy. "I've wanted to kiss you like that since the first time I saw you."

He sighs against my neck and pulls me closer. I trace his tattoos with my fingertips. "I don't want to lose you," he says quietly, pulling back to look at me.

I meet his dark eyes. "You won't."

5 DAYS

I want to live.

Ten days ago, I was resigned to die. I'd accepted my fate, knowing there was nothing I could do about it. Then I met Mace, and he told me that there *was* something I could do. He told me I could fight. Mace gives me hope. He makes me want to try. He makes me want to live.

I hear voices downstairs. I'm still wearing the clothes from yesterday. They smell stale and smoky, but I have nothing else.

I enter Miles's living room to find him with Dad and Mace, watching the Reports.

"Look. We made the news," Dad says.

I frown and perch on the edge of the sofa.

"Crime will not be tolerated. Not now, not ever," the voice-over says. The footage shows our house burning. It's hard to look, but I can't avert my eyes.

"Rebels are among you. The images you see on your screens are the consequences of rebellion against the New World. Against our future," the woman's voice continues.

"Sector seven has now been locked down: no more power, no more water, no more citizen collections. If you received an

invitation for the New World, that invitation is no longer valid. The clock, however, will remain on until Day Zero and curfew is still in effect."

My stomach drops. "Turn it off," I say. Miles clicks the TV off and the room falls silent. "What do we do?"

Dad runs a hand through his hair, making it spike up. He looks like he hasn't slept. Sighing heavily, he says, "I don't know. If we leave the house, they'll see us on the cameras. I'm supposed to be training at the high school again this morning."

"We should still go," I say. "We can't just sit here and wait for the clock to hit zero. We need to prepare, and to share the information we have with the rest of the group."

"But the cameras—"

"We'll avoid them! We can split up and take the back streets for as far as we can. Cover our faces. We *have* to try," I say.

"She's right, Len," Miles says.

"It's a risk," Dad says. "A big one."

"What other choice do we have?" I ask.

We raid Miles's closet for baseball caps that'll hide our faces. Mace and Miles are fine to walk through the streets, so it's only Dad and me that need to be disguised.

While the others make plans, I pick up Miles's phone to call Kyra. There's no dial tone and then I remember the power's been cut.

Kyra didn't call me back after I left the message about Mom last week. She didn't care at all. It hurts worse when

I think of every time I worried about her and her family. But I'm still worried about her. I slam the phone down and wait in the kitchen for Dad.

Mace and Miles leave first, heading to the high school so they're present when the group starts to arrive. Dad and I go out the kitchen window and shuffle between the backs of the houses again. When we come to a street to cross, we wait, sometimes for a long time, until the cameras are pointing the other way. Then we dash across and continue on through the back alleys. It's exhausting.

There are more people in the high school gym than last time. Mace is waiting for me by the doors when we arrive. He waits until Dad disappears in the crowd, then smiles and kisses me. Dad's fine with us being together, but we're respectful around him.

"You made it," Mace says, pulling my cap from my head. I look around at all the new faces. "Your dad's been recruiting heavily," he adds as we walk hand-in-hand through the crowd.

Cass knocks into me, hard. "The wanderer returns!" she says, smirking.

Dad's already standing on a bench, with Remy and Miles on either side of him. He gestures for Mace and me to join him. I look out at the group: some are sitting on the shiny floor, or on the benches at the sides, and others stay standing.

"I'm sure Miles has informed you of what happened to my home." There's a wave of nodding heads. "That doesn't mean the same will happen to you. No one knows what we are doing—I can assure you all that the reason for the fire was due to something else." He unscrews the sketches I did of the machines and hands them out. "Please, pass these around."

The first person he hands the paper to, a boy around my age, stares at it for a long time. "What is this?" he says.

"That," Dad says, "is a cyborg."

The boy drops the piece of paper, and the woman next to him picks it up, studies it, and passes it on.

"There have been some . . . developments," Dad continues.

"How did you get this?" Cass shouts from the back of the room. She's waving the sketch in the air.

"Sia, why don't you explain this to everyone," Dad says.

What? Me? My mouth dries up as a few dozen pairs of eyes zone in on me.

"Th-there are only a f-few things you need to know," I begin. I clear my throat and take a breath. "First, they're drawn to human life. You can run from them, but you can't hide. They will sense you and they will find you. We can't outrun them forever, so every machine must be destroyed as quickly as possible.

"Second, they crush people. I watched one of the cyborgs crush a man to death. Only when he was dead did the machine let go. Don't let them get hold of you. Their fingers are like knives, and they will rip right through your skin."

"How do *you* know all of this?" Cass says, her eyes narrowing.

"I already said," I snap. "I *saw* them."

Worried murmuring breaks out among the group. They're right to fret. It's human versus machine. Soft flesh versus hard metal. We're training to fight for our lives, and they're programmed to kill and leave no survivors. And they've done just that in six other sectors. The Reports show human bodies ripped apart; blood splattered across gray walls; body parts burning in the fires, or buried under ash and rubble. The machines are designed to cause that level of destruction.

Dad claps his hands together. "Come on, come on. This is a good thing."

"*How exactly?*" Cass says.

"We know what we're fighting now," Dad says.

"Sure, but look at it," she says, holding the sheet up above her head. The others in the room turn to look at her, at the sketch, and the silence tells me everything I need to know. They're terrified.

Dad scowls. "We're going to start training," he says. "We've wasted enough time already."

"Yeah." She looks at me. "We have."

We split into groups and begin our warm-up exercises. It's a slow start, as everyone's out of the habit after missing a few sessions and spirits are low after seeing the sketches of the cyborgs and hearing what they can do. But Dad's resilient, doing everything he can to keep up morale.

I hope it's enough.

The day drags.

A lot of people approach me, asking questions about the cyborgs and the New World. I take time to answer every one of them, which means I miss quite a bit of training with all of the interruptions.

Dad, Miles, and Remy are bent over the cyborg sketch, talking in hushed voices. I catch snippets of conversation when I move to train near them, but not enough. I want to know what's going on.

"What are you talking about?" I ask, squeezing into a gap between Dad and Miles.

"New training exercises now that we have more of an idea of what we're up against," Dad says.

"I can help," I offer. I take the sketch. "It's important not to let them get hold of you, so we should practice dodging them. They're fast as well, so we need to be able to move quickly to avoid them."

We continue to discuss the machines and I help the three of them create new tasks for tomorrow. Training is long finished by the time we're done. We stay until dark, making plans for Day Zero—we'll round all the sector's citizens up and lead them to the hill, then those of us with weapons who are trained to fight will form a perimeter and pick the machines off one by one.

I look at my drawing of the cyborg again, remembering its sharp fingers and hollow eyes. Then I look at all the notes we've written and feel a tiny spark of hope.

4 DAYS

Mace is gone.

He slept in Miles's spare room with me last night, our bodies pressed together under the duvet on the twin bed. Mace had given me a clean T-shirt from his backpack, which reaches down to my knees, and Dad said one of the women would be bringing me a spare set of clothes to today's training session.

Mace is no longer beside me, though. The side of the bed he slept on is cold. I scramble out from under the covers and start to pull my jeans on when he walks into the room. "Hi," he says.

Mace crosses the room and slides his arms around my waist, gently pulling me against him. I laugh and bury my head into the space between his neck and shoulder. "Miles is making some food for us," he says. "We're not eating enough, and we need our strength for these training sessions."

"Okay," I say. "I'll go get ready."

In the bathroom, I squirt some toothpaste onto my finger and rub it over my teeth. Miles has set out four bottles of water—one for each of us—and that's all we have. I mix a little with some soap and wash as best as I can with it. My reluctance to use much water to wash the soap off leaves my skin a little sticky, but at least I smell clean.

After we eat, the four of us set out for training again. Mace and Miles go ahead, and Dad and I sneak in the tight space behind houses and rush through streets. I'm wearing my jeans, boots, Mace's oversize T-shirt that I slept in last night, and my jacket over it. I can't wait to get some clean clothes.

On entering the high school gym, I immediately notice that our numbers have decreased significantly.

"This isn't good," I say when Mace comes to meet me by the double doors.

Mace's friend Pax is with him. He's eighteen, the same age as Mace. Pax has short blonde hair. His skin is smooth, his features chiseled and sharp.

"So, where is everyone?" I ask.

"A lot haven't come back after yesterday," Mace says.

"They're scared," Pax adds.

"What will leaving us achieve? It only lessens their chance of survival if they don't fight with us," I say.

"You're right," Pax says. "Maybe they'll realize that before it's too late."

"Come on." Mace holds my hand. "Let's focus on the people who *are* here."

Evasion.

"Dodge, avoid, escape. Once a machine has hold of you, it won't let go. Not until you're dead. Don't be caught by them. *Evade* them," Dad calls out as he paces the gym, weaving between clusters of people.

Reflexes.

"Reflexes must be sharp and fast. We must be aware at all times of everything that is happening around us. Be ready to strike."

Putting the new training into effect, we pair together for one-on-one exercises. We take turns being either a machine or a human for the training. I pair up with Mace. Pax, unfortunately, pairs with Cass, and they come to train beside us.

Mace is the machine. He reaches for my face, his hand clawed. I move my head to the side, and his hand shoots past my ear. He smiles. "Good!"

I bounce from foot to foot, waiting for his next move. He lunges at me with both arms. I jump back, but I'm a second too late and his fingers brush my sides. If he really were a cyborg I'd be bleeding all over the floor. I freeze in shock when I realize that, and Mace launches at me again. This time, his arms wrap around my waist and we fall backward onto the soft mats on the floor.

I grunt when we land. "No!"

"Sia, it's okay," Mace says, supporting himself on his arms.

"No, it's not, Mace! This is me, dead."

"We only just started training like this. You'll pick it up, I know you will."

"In four days?" I say.

He offers me a half smile. "In four days," he parrots. He kisses me, and I sink into the cushion pad below me.

"What are you trying to do?" Cass says. "Kill her with kisses?"

Mace lifts himself off me and I see her standing over us with a nasty smirk on her face.

"Leave them alone," Pax says.

"How about we switch?" she says to Mace. "I'll be Sia's machine, and you be Pax's."

"I don't think—"

"It's all right," I say, standing up. "I'll pair up with Cass." I know she won't hold back and I see it as a good challenge.

Cass narrows her eyes and crouches. "Ready?" she says, then swipes at me before I have a chance to respond. She squats low and swings her leg out at mine, trying to knock me off my feet. I jump, bending my knees into a tuck.

"They don't do that!" I say, but she ignores me and tries again. I leap off the ground and she fails to make contact for a second time. I land awkwardly. "They *don't* do that," I repeat, angry now. The machines use their arms to crush a body to death. They don't try to trip people.

"Don't care," Cass says, then punches me in the stomach. I stagger back but I don't fall, even though she's knocked the air from my lungs. "And. That. Is. Payback," she says, dusting her knuckles and smiling triumphantly.

I stand and wait for her to come at me again. "Is that it?" I say.

Cass snarls and clears the distance between us in two quick steps. I duck as she lashes out at my face and my hands connect with her middle. I push her backward, but she doesn't go far. Her face is red and she's panting. Her hands whip out for my face again and I jump to the side. She screeches with frustration.

"That's enough!" Dad says beside us. Cass doesn't stop. She grabs for my hair, and I dig my nails into her flesh. Dad pulls Cass back and calls for a break. I'm furious now. I don't want him to protect me like that. What if he's not there to help me when we're fighting the cyborgs for real?

Cass storms through the double doors and off into the dark halls alone. "Ten minutes!" Dad calls after her. "Wow. You sure rattled her cage."

"Dad," I hiss, guiding him to one side. "Don't do that."

"Do what?" he asks, a genuine look of puzzlement on his face.

"Come to my rescue like that."

"But you're my daughter!"

"I'm not a child! I can take care of myself."

He holds out his hands. "All right, all right. Is everything okay over here, though?"

"Yes. I can handle it." I want to fight with Cass. It's the best training I could have here. I get the feeling that no one else would hurt me. With Cass, it's real.

"We're working in larger groups after break. You'll be with Cass, Pax, and Mace."

I smile. *Good.*

Dad goes around the room, talking to others and assigning groups for the next exercise. It's not much different than the first, but we practice one human against three cyborgs this time. I'm the human first—by Cass's suggestion. I'm down within seconds. Over and over and over. I dodge one and another gets me. It's impossible. Everyone else tries and no one manages to avoid a hit. Mace lasts longer than all of us, but eventually Pax tackles him and it's game over.

Hours and hours of these exercises go by, and I don't feel like I'm getting any better. When the day is called to an end, I'm exhausted.

I wait on the benches while Dad, Miles, and Mace get ready to leave. Dad finishes up by explaining the Day Zero plan to the group and I sit and think of the gym class Kyra and I had first thing every Wednesday morning. Gym class was the only real exercise we got and I looked forward to it. I wonder what Kyra would think of this group. I wonder if she'd want to join if I told her about it.

Back at Miles's, I go upstairs to wash and change into the pajamas one of the women brought to training for me. I was given a clean white T-shirt and a pair of black jeans, too.

Mace waits for me in the spare room while I change in the bathroom. Dad and Miles let him stay here and sleep in the bed with me as long as we leave the door open. I'm not even sure where Mace lived before we came here. Where he spent his time when we weren't together.

I reenter the bedroom and Mace is lying on the bed, resting on one elbow. My middle warms as I slowly walk toward him. He watches me with his dark eyes.

I slip into bed beside him, lying flat on my back, then he moves himself on top of me and my breath catches.

"Is this okay?" he whispers against my neck. I nod. He holds himself over me, leaning on his elbows like he did in the gym, covering me with his body. All I can feel is his warmth. All I can smell is the crisp herbal soap we both used in the bathroom, mixed with minty toothpaste. All I can see is *him*.

Mace kisses my neck slowly. He traces my jawline with his lips and works his way along until he finds mine. My lips part and my body trembles beneath his. I slip my hands around his back, pulling him closer still, until there's no space left between us.

We move apart at the sound of footsteps on the stairs. Mace lowers himself down beside me, draping one arm over my stomach, and we close our eyes.

Dad pauses outside the door. I hear him move on and the bathroom door click shut. I turn my head on the pillow so that I'm facing Mace. He kisses me softly and whispers, "Good night," against my lips.

3 DAYS

I'm back at the high school gym for another day of training.

Dad's increased the hours for those who can stay. We're getting so close now.

So close.

In the morning we do human versus machine training again. I'm still no better at it. I can hold off getting caught for longer now, but eventually Mace or Cass or whoever I'm partnered with takes me down.

After a short break, we move on to a new exercise. We're learning to hit a moving target. This'll be helpful if we can perfect our aim as it means we won't need to get too close to the machine. I doubt we can take out any cyborg with what we have, but there's a chance we could disorientate it, knock it off its feet, or damage it in some way before it approaches.

I have the hammer from Dad's toolbox on the belt loop of my jeans. I've become comfortable with the weight of it there, the feel of it pressed against my thigh. Aside from the weapons some of us keep close, there's a bench in the gym displaying objects we've collected as a group. It's pitiful, really: pipes, shovels, household tools. How much damage can these things really do? But this is all we have—other than the few guns handed out to select people—so we have to make the most of them.

Dad, Remy, and Miles went around the high school collecting wheeled chairs from the classrooms and offices for this next session. Dad and Remy stand against one wall of the gym and push the chairs across the floor. We take turns throwing objects at them and Miles records how we do.

I had fourteen tries in total: nine hits and five misses. Mace had fourteen tries, too: eleven hits and three misses.

Morning flies into afternoon, and afternoon to evening, and the group starts to filter out and return to their homes. Another day gone. Another day closer to zero.

Mace and I sit together in the corner of the gym, waiting for Miles and Dad to finish a few things before heading home.

"Mace," I say. "Where do you live?"

He tenses, then looks at me out of the corner of his eye. "I live with you guys."

"Yeah, but what about before?"

"Why do you want to know?" he says, and there's a guarded tone to his voice.

I shrug. "I'm just curious."

He sighs heavily and spins a wrench around in his hand. "I didn't live anywhere, really," he finally answers.

"You must have. No one in the sector is homeless, Mace."

"Well, I am, but I wasn't always. It happened a few days before I met you. After that, I stayed with some of the guys, like Pax or Remy, but never anywhere for too long. They have families, and it's a hard time for everyone. I'm sure they didn't care too much having a houseguest. Other nights, I just slept here in the high school, or anywhere else I could find."

My stomach churns. "*Why?*"

He looks at me, stops spinning the wrench. "My mom, she . . . she died a couple days after we found out that the sector would be attacked. She was . . . she couldn't . . . she took—" His voice catches, but I have a feeling I know what he's about to say. He's about to tell me that she was inconsolable, that she couldn't handle it, couldn't sit and wait for the brutal death the machines would bring. That she took her own life. Just like my mom did.

"Mine too," I whisper. Mace opens his mouth to speak, but I cut him off. I don't want to talk about Mom. Not here, not now. "What about your dad?" I ask.

Mace hesitates for a moment, then continues. "Dad, he was adamant that we weren't to leave the house. He said that he and I should hide and wait for it all to blow over. But I wouldn't do it, wouldn't stay and hide with him, and he didn't like that. He watched the Reports, he got angry, he was eaten up with grief over my mom's death. Despite me telling him time and time again that I wasn't just going to hunker down and hide, he still tried to convince me to stay locked up with him. He said it was just the two of us now and that we needed each other to survive this. When I still wouldn't do as he asked, he threw me out. I was angry at first, and then decided to give him time to cool

197

off before I went back home. Only, when I got back, he'd
boarded up the house."

I reach out and hold Mace's free hand. His other is back
to flipping the wrench over and over again. He gives me a
small appreciative smile.

"I kept going back. He spoke to me, shouted at me
and told me to go away. Then, after a while, he stopped
responding to my knocks and my pleas. I go there every
day, but he hasn't spoken to me for nineteen days now. I
don't even know if he's alive."

"Shouldn't you want to go inside and check?" I say.
"We can go together and break in." As I make the offer,
my throat pulses. I imagine what we'd find—his dad in a
dark, unventilated house with his wife's corpse. I shudder
and Mace squeezes my hand.

"I can't," he whispers, shaking his head.

"You must wonder, though? What he's doing, what he's
thinking, what he's feeling?"

"Every day," Mace says.

"Then we need to go. You need to have some sort of
closure."

He shakes his head. "I don't. Everything's fine now,
everything's all right. I don't want to ruin that. I was so
angry, Sia. But then your dad found me and told me about
his plan. At first, I just wanted to fight as a way to get rid
of all the pain built up inside me. I had nothing left to lose
and I didn't care if I died. I just wanted to fight. But now
I've met you, and now I have something to live for again.
I don't need to go back home. You're all I want. I'll do

everything I can to keep us both alive. *Everything.* I can't lose you."

Mace pulls me into a hug and rubs my back.

Back at Miles's house, I sit on the twin bed alone in the dark.

I can't stop thinking about Mace's dad. Nineteen days he's been shut up in his house without speaking a word to Mace. Nineteen days Mace has visited, desperate to hear his father's voice.

"Hey," Mace says as he enters the bedroom, easing me back against the wall. He kisses me, slowly, softly.

I don't kiss him back, though.

"Mace," I say, putting my hand on his chest.

He pulls back. "What's wrong?"

"What if he's alive? What if he's suffering? I can't stop thinking about it."

Mace sighs. "My dad? Sia, we talked about this. I'm not going to break into my house."

"I could go for you if you want me to."

"No way. Look, I appreciate that you're concerned, but I'm not doing it."

"When was the last time you tried to speak with him?"

"Yesterday," he says. "I circled the house, I called out for him, and I banged my fist against the boards. Nothing happened. He isn't alive. I know he isn't."

"But what if he is?"

"He *isn't*, Sia," Mace snaps. "Please, just drop it."

"I will if you take me there."

"Sia—"

"Just take me, Mace. You might not need to know, but I do."

"You don't even know him! Why are you so desperate to find out if my dad's alive or not?"

"Because you have a chance to save him. I did nothing to save my mom. I didn't know what she'd done until it was too late. If it were her in that house, I'd have broken in a long time ago. I'd give anything for a second chance."

Mace's skin pales. He reaches out for me but I flinch away from his touch. I haven't spoken about my mom like this to anyone. I've never felt that I could. Then the words come tumbling out of my mouth, just like that. So freely, so easily.

Mace bows his head. "Len told some of us what'd happened to his wife. When I found out you were his daughter . . ."

"You've known for that long?" I say. My heart drums in my ears, pounding so loudly that I can hardly hear what he's saying. Dad discussed Mom's death with *Mace*. With Miles and Remy, and who knows who else. But he didn't even speak with me about it. No time other than the morning after it happened. And I've held it all inside, have suffered alone, until now.

"I'm really sorry," Mace says.

I shake my head. "Let's just go."

It's dark out.

Three hours until curfew. Mace and I walk quickly through empty streets. There's no light other than the slightest

hint of red from the clock tower. The darkness serves to protect me from the cameras, but it's not enough cover that I
can walk freely in the middle of the streets without risk. I still
take precautions, even at this hour.

Mace's house is just as I imagined. Wooden boards
cover the windows and doors. The house is dark, silent,
lifeless. Mace knocks on the boards, shouting to his dad
like he knows I want him to. When no answer comes, he
shrugs. "See." I pull a crowbar from my belt. "Where did
you get that?" he asks.

I raise my eyebrows, though I'm not sure he can see
me clearly in the darkness, and pass him the crowbar. He
takes it from me and turns it over in his hand. Blowing out
a puff of air, he walks back to the house and uses the tool
to pry away the wooden board covering one of the front
windows. Some of the wood chips and snaps away under
the force, creating a small hole in one corner. Mace curses.
"The shutters are locked," he says.

"They don't lock until curfew, so they must just be
closed. Push it open," I say.

He smashes the window and hits the shutter. He drops the
crowbar and sticks his head through the gap. He tries to squeeze
himself through the hole but his shoulders are too broad.

"Damn it," he says, pulling himself back out and picking up the crowbar.

"I'll go," I say, eyeing the gap. "I can fit through there."

"No, Sia, I don't want you—"

"It's fine, Mace. Really. I'll unlock the door once I'm
inside."

Reluctantly, Mace helps push me through the hole and into the house. I suck in a breath when I slice my palm on a piece of glass. I hold the injured hand to my chest once I get to my feet. Inside the house is pitch-dark.

I reach my hand back through the gap and Mace passes the crowbar to me. There's a faint smell of something rotting, which I take to be the garbage. Or Mace's mom. Trying to put that thought out of my mind, I feel my way through the room until I find a door.

I open it and the rotten odor slams into me.

It coats my tongue, seeps down my throat, claws its way up my nasal passage. It clouds every sense and takes over so absolutely that I have to fight to stay on my feet.

I'm frozen, blinking in the blackness. I can't see. I can't move. I swallow, hard, and choke on the horror. Dead things. Festering, decaying, rotting in this house. With trembling hands, I feel my way to the front door. I don't want to let Mace in here now, but his dad could still be alive. I'm just too afraid to call out his name and check.

I find the front door and lodge the crowbar beneath it, pulling at the weak nails Mace's dad has hammered into the wood. Once the panel breaks away, I push it to the side so that I can open the front door.

Mace steps inside before I have a chance to warn him.

He lifts his sleeve to cover his nose and mouth and staggers back. I crave clean air and follow him outside. The red hue the clock tower casts on us reflects over Mace's eyes. They shine wet.

"I *told* you," he says, leaning back against the outside wall.

"You don't know for sure that it's him. Your mom, she's in there, but—"

"I'm not going back inside. He's gone. They both are. Can't you accept it now that you've been in there and seen—smelled—what's inside for yourself?"

My breath hitches. I feel a pulse of guilt for what I've done; it beats and throbs and roars in my ears. "Mace, I'm sorry."

"Let's just go home," he says. He leans his head back and looks up at the house. "Did you see anything while you were inside?"

I swallow the lump that's swelled in my throat. "No," I say. "It's too dark." Mace pushes off the wall, wraps me in his arms, and buries his head in my jacket. "I'm sorry. I should never have made you come here."

"Just take me away," he says, his words muffled against my shoulder. "Please."

The clock tower beeps ten times, warning anyone out on the streets that there are only two hours left until curfew. We move away from the house, my arm wrapped tightly around Mace, and head back through the darkness.

2 DAYS

It's the calm before the storm.

We finish up training in the afternoon. Dad goes easy on us today, urging the group to spend time with family and friends. Tomorrow will be a long, hard day—the last day. I think of visiting Kyra, but I can't face her family. She didn't return my call. She doesn't want to see me. I need to let go.

Mace and I head to the lake. There are no cameras on the hill and around the water, so it's like a different place. It's like I'm not in the sector anymore. Like I'm out in the Rough, free.

We sit on the crisp grass and watch the wind ripple the surface of the lake. We're quiet. We don't have much time left and the pressure to savor this moment stuns me into silence. This is it. This one afternoon is all I have left before the training and the fighting takes over everything.

Mace breaks the silence. "Do you know how to use a gun?" He's sitting a little away from me and the distance is excruciating. I want to be near him, now more than ever. I shake my head; I've never even held a gun. "Come on," he says, getting to his feet. "I'll show you."

We both stand, and Mace positions me in front of him. His chest presses up against my spine. His strong arms slip around me, and he places his gun in my hands.

With his hands on my hips, he maneuvers me into a shooting stance and tells me where to put my feet. "Feet and shoulders apart," he says, but I'm having a hard time concentrating on his words with his arms around me like this. "Arms straight. Good." The gun feels heavy in my hand. "Choose your target, but keep your finger off the trigger."

"Why?"

"You're not going to shoot. I don't have enough bullets for you to practice actually shooting."

"Okay," I say, letting my arms droop a little.

"Keep your arms straight and locked, Sia. And your feet need to be planted firmly on the ground," Mace says. My arms and legs ache while he teaches me the proper stance, grip, aim, and control. He smiles once we're done. "That was good," he says. "Now you know what to do, just in case."

"In case of what?"

"In case anything happens to me. You take my gun and—"

"Let's not talk about that," I say, holding my hand up, palm out. "I don't want to think about that today."

Mace shrugs off his jacket and lifts his shirt over his head. I drink in his firm, smooth torso and his tattooed chest.

"What are you doing?" I ask.

He reaches for me and takes the gun from my hand, then places it on the ground with his shirt. He takes the zipper of my jacket in his hands and slowly opens it, then guides the coat over my shoulders and down my arms until it drops to the ground by my feet. His fingers skim the hem of my T-shirt and my breath catches. He runs his hands softly over my bare skin and leans in close. His lips are against mine.

"Do you want to go for a swim?" he breathes. Still holding the hem of my shirt, he teases me toward the lake.

He eases himself in first, then holds his arms out to me. I hardly notice the cold. All I see and feel is Mace.

He pushes off and we glide across the water. My arms are around his neck. His arms are around my waist, holding me to him. My forehead rests on his and he closes his eyes.

We stop moving through the water and hold each other, bobbing up and down. Mace lifts one hand out of the water, still supporting my waist with the other. He brings his hand to my neck, his thumb fitting behind my ear, pinching the lobe. He opens his eyes and looks at me, then slowly brings me closer.

His lips meet mine and I melt. My insides are electric. My heart pummels my ribcage. Beneath the surface, I wrap my legs around him and he holds me tighter. My chin goes underwater and I break away, afraid we might drown. Mace smiles and guides us back to the water's edge.

He lifts me out of the lake and climbs out behind me. He eases me back onto the grass. My eyes search his, and his lips find mine again and again and again. I'm breathless, smoldering, aching for more. I never want to stop.

But the day is turning to night. It's almost over.

1 DAY

It's past curfew and nobody's home.

Earlier, Mace went back to the high school to help Dad, Miles, and Remy set up for the last day of training. He said they might not make it back before curfew, but I hoped they would.

The house is black. The shutters are locked, cutting off any and all light. The power's been out for days, all but the clock and shutters. It never seemed to bother me when the house was full. Now that I'm alone here, though, the house has transformed into something from nightmares.

I remember being at Mace's house—the smell, the fear, the darkness.

I'm laying on the twin bed, still fully clothed. The house is totally silent. The whole sector is. The hammer on my belt loop digs into my side. I sit up to unzip my boots and kick them off. I can't sleep, so I stare into the blackness and think about nothing.

A dull noise somewhere in the distance cuts through the silence so suddenly that I'm certain it's only my imagination. But then it sounds again, and again—a heavy thudding sound every couple of seconds.

I sit upright and put my boots back on, catching my leg in the zipper as I hurry. As I reach the bedroom door, there's an explosion of chaos downstairs.

I pull the hammer from my belt and swing the bedroom door open. Standing at the top of the stairs, I see a faint light seeping through an enormous hole in the side of the house. The metal shutters are shredded, hanging from the window like ribbons. The wall is dust on the floor.

Heavy footsteps get louder, closer, and a cyborg comes into view. It's at the bottom of the stairs. I almost lose it as I stand face-to-face with the machine again, nothing but air between us this time.

It stamps up the steps, fast and sure. I place my shaking hands on the walls framing the staircase and kick it in the jaw once it comes close enough. It swings out its arm and nicks me with its sharp fingers. I yelp, but it's only a scratch.

The machine falls back down the stairs. *Thump, thump, thump.* The back of its neck hits hard against the edge of one of the steps and its head snaps off. I run down the stairs and jump over its twitching body.

I climb through the hole in the wall and out into the street. The clock is off, no longer displaying its numbers. With the red glare from the clock tower gone, the moon and stars are the only source of light.

I look directly above me and all I see is metal.

It's an oddly beautiful, yet terrifying sight. Framed by stars, the machines, attached to parachutes, glide down gracefully from the sky and land in the sector with a heavy thud.

But it's too soon, I think.

Then it hits me: *they know*.

The New World knows what we've been doing. They're trying to catch us off guard, and they've succeeded. Nobody is ready. Everyone's at home after taking the afternoon off, tucked up in their beds, unaware, unprepared.

I'm dizzy, but now is not the time to be weak or afraid. So I start running, hard and fast, through the streets, heading for the high school. My lungs burn and my legs ache, but I ignore the pain.

Thud.

Right beside me a machine lands. I watch as it rips through the walls of a house.

Thud.

I skid to a stop as one drops right in front of me. The parachute flops like a fish above it. I grab the material out of the air, then wrap it tightly around the machine until it's completely covered and tangled in the white sheet. I shove the machine hard, and it falls to the side. I lift my hammer and bring it down over and over. A scream works its way out of my body, rattling my spine, vibrating in my fingertips. I bring the hammer down one last time. Then I'm running again.

When I reach the school, I find blood on the stairs leading up to the main door. I enter cautiously, hammer raised in front of me. The machines don't react to sound or anything other than your presence, so I start calling out for Dad and Mace.

My heart leaps when I push through another set of doors into a dim corridor. A long trail of blood leads to the gym. Lining the walls of the corridor, the lockers are stained with handprints and bloody smudges, like someone's dragged themself along the floor using the lockers as support.

I find myself standing in front of my own locker. It is covered in stickers and little notes from my friends, and now has a new addition of fresh blood. I run my hand over where Kyra had written *Best Friends Forever*. I'd give anything for it to be a regular school day, surrounded by friends and teachers, rather than walking alone through empty corridors not knowing if I'll even be alive when the sun rises.

I step cautiously into the gym, coming to the end of the blood trail. Inside, a man lies face down, his blood pooling around his middle. One of his arms is missing, and I can see it only feet away from him.

I cover my nose and mouth and will myself not to be sick. It's one thing seeing gruesome scenes on the Reports, and another experiencing them in real life. On the TV screen, you can't see the details of the detached body parts. Here, I see splintered bone, blackened by blood and surrounded by soft, ripped flesh. Here, I see the thick flow of blood bubbling from the still arm. Here, a coppery scent overwhelms me. I rub my hands over my eyes, feeling light-headed again.

The man groans. He's still alive. I crouch down but keep my distance.

"Hey," I say, my voice trembling. "A-are you awake?"

"Mm," he mumbles, swiping his face across the floor so he can see me. "Sia?" he says.

"It's me, I'm here," I reply. But I don't know who he is.

"You need to get out of here. Your dad, he's—"

His breath hitches and his eyes go wide. I'm suddenly afraid the next word is going to be *dead*.

"He's what? Where is he?"

"Run," he croaks, hoarse and strained. "*Run!*" he then screams with his last breath.

I turn in time to miss the mechanical hand that's reaching for me. It reaches out again, grabbing hold of my jacket sleeve. I scream and jerk away. Its fist clamps around the material, its other arm swinging for me. I pull, hard, causing the fabric to rip.

Free from its hold, I stumble onto the floor. Feeling something warm and sticky beneath me, I look down to see I've fallen into fresh blood. I'm covered in it, and the strong metallic smell fills my nostrils. I gag. With all my effort, I push to my feet and take off toward the nearest exit. I have to get out of the building.

I run through a door that leads to the schoolyard—a big open space—instead of back into the dark corridors.

In the distance, I hear banging and screaming and the roar of fire. *It's started.*

Across the gravel, I see three silhouettes.

"*Dad!*" I yell. My voice carries loudly across the open ground.

He runs to me. "Sia, are you alone?" Before I can answer, he looks down and sees the blood painting my hands and soaked into my T-shirt. He gasps. "Are you hurt?"

"No. It's not my blood," I say grimly. "There's a man inside the gym. He's dead. And the machine is still inside the school."

Dad curses. "Get ready," he calls over to two other figures in the distance. As they approach, I can see their features and my stomach plummets. It's Remy and Miles.

I grab Dad's arm. "Where's Mace?"

"He went back to the house for you."

"No," I breathe. "Dad, we have to go after him. If he's alone—"

"He's got Pax with him. He'll be all right," Dad says, putting his hand on my shoulder. "He's the best fighter we've got. If anyone can survive this it's him."

I nod and look back at the school. I know that Mace is strong, but how strong is he against these machines? But there's no time to think as the school door flies open, and four cyborgs spill out of the gym.

"Shit." Dad roughly pushes me behind him as he, Remy, and Miles step forward, guns aimed. "Sia, stay back," he commands.

"I can help! I know the training."

"No. Stay back!"

I hold the hammer in my hand, firm and steady. I think of the cyborg I kicked down the stairs, knocking its head off. I think of the machine I wrapped in its own parachute and pummeled with this hammer. I draw on the energy, on the anger, on the hate, and move out from behind my dad, to stand ready for what's to come.

Miles takes the lead, running toward the approaching cyborgs. He points his gun at a machine, aims, fires. The force of the bullet knocks the machine to the ground, but the bullet ricochets off its body and embeds itself in Miles's skull instead. I scream and cover my mouth as he falls back and lies motionless. Miles and the machine lay side by side. The hard, metal body is still moving, though, while the soft body, *Miles's* body, remains still. The cyborg can't get up. It scratches at the ground and spins around, like a tortoise turned upside-down.

The door opens again. Mace, Pax and another man run out into the yard. Relief washes over me. *He's alive.*

Mace's eyes find mine, fierce and filled with relief. The three of them circle the machines and take their places next to Dad and Remy. There are six of us now, and three machines.

I bounce from foot to foot, waiting to strike. Mace covers my body with his. I step out from behind him.

"Mace, I don't need you to save me. I just need you fighting beside me."

He nods, but his expression is pained. "Be careful, Sia. This is real now."

The machines are closing in. A couple more seconds and they'll be close enough to reach out for us, and they won't stop coming until we're dead.

Or until we destroy them.

I remember my training. So when a cyborg reaches for me, I duck down and move to its side. Then I swing my hammer so it connects with the back of its head.

The cyborg reaches out again and, this time, its hand encounters flesh.

"No!" I shout.

The man who arrived with Mace and Pax is locked in the machine's grasp.

"No!" I yell again. He cries out in shock as the machine clamps its metal arms around his waist and lifts him off the ground.

I hit at it again, but I'm too distracted and dizzy from the scent of blood and metal so I barely dent its exterior. The machine moves its arms inward, crushing. My mind flashes back to the New World, to when I saw Mr. Tanner killed in this same way. I can't watch that happen again. *I can't.*

We have only seconds to stop the cyborg before the man dies. Circles of blood expand on his white shirt as metal fingers pierce his skin. This is all too familiar. His cries become gurgled as blood pours from his open mouth and I hear his bones snap. I know I can't save him now, but I hit at the back of the cyborg's skull over and over until it starts to break.

A bullet bounces off the machine's side. I stop hitting and look to see who's shooting. Mace is approaching, arm extended, gun aimed. He shoots again.

"*Mace!* No!"

I launch at him and his third bullet fires into the sky.

"What are you *doing?*" he screams at me over the noise.

"The bullets bounce. Miles shot one and the bullet ricocheted off the metal and hit him in the head. Don't use your gun."

Without a word, he shoves the gun back into the waist of his jeans and unhooks the crowbar hanging from his belt. I take it from him and finish the job I started on the machine.

Its head is already lolling to the side. I shove the curved end of the crowbar into the back of the cyborg's neck and pull. Sparks erupt as I yank the weapon back out along with a net of wires. The machine's grip loosens on the dead man and the body drops. It lands with a thump to the ground, bones protruding from the man's chest where they'd been pushed together and broken. The headless body of the machine falls, too.

I stand in shock, staring at the gruesome body on the ground.

"Sia, watch out!" Dad shouts from across the yard. I turn and come face-to-face with another machine. It swings out its arm and the movement knocks the crowbar from my hand. I leap back as it lunges for me and fumble at my waist for the hammer. I pull at it, but it's stuck on my belt hook and won't come free.

The cyborg knocks me off my feet. A scream tears from my throat as I hit the hard ground. My vision dances, black dots scatter before my eyes. My head throbs where I hit it and blood soaks the back, sticky and matting in my hair.

I scramble backward, using my hands to propel my body away from the machine. But for each movement I make, it does, too. Each long stride closes the gap between us.

I kick the gravel beneath my boots, sending little flecks spraying all over the cyborg's legs. Small clangs echo around me as the pebbles hit metal.

The machine reaches for me again. Its long, cold, razor-like fingers slash across my face. Then I feel the warmth of my blood as it rises to the surface through the cuts.

Pax is suddenly in front of me, smashing a shovel against the machine's middle. It staggers back with the force of the blow.

Then there is Mace, putting his arms around me, his shirt torn and dark with sweat and his hair stuck to his temples. He pulls me to my feet just in time to see Pax slam the shovel into the cyborg's neck and slice its head half off. The cyborg loses its footing. Its head hangs to the side, wires exposed and flickering. Then it stops moving and crashes to the ground.

I'm breathing hard and heavy. I use my jeans to rub the gravel from my hands, which are dented with the pattern of tiny stones. Pax claps me on the shoulder.

I hear shouting and spin around to see that Dad and Remy have taken down the final machine in the yard and are now rushing toward us, shouting for us to run.

More cyborgs are coming out of the gym, splattered with human blood and smudged with soot. Their sharp fingertips drip black blood. I wiggle my hammer from my belt hook, and the five of us sprint away.

The sector's streets are not a good place to fight. The space is cramped when empty and now people are spilling out of their houses, pushing past each other in their desperate attempt to escape the machines. There are uncontrolled fires spreading fast throughout the neighborhood, and thick smoke in the air makes it difficult to see and breathe.

A gut-wrenching scream pierces my ears and I turn to see Cass laying face-down in the street. Her arms are sprawled out in front of her and she's trying to grab hold of whatever she can. The machine that stands over her has its skeletal hand clamped around her leg, its fingers piercing her skin. Cass's cries are desperate. She's pleading for someone to help her. *This shouldn't be happening to her. She's a good fighter. We weren't prepared for this tonight.*

I run toward her, holding the hammer firmly in both hands. I take a swing at the machine, but barely knock it sideways. I look into its unseeing eyes and jab the end of the hammer into one. It knocks its head back in a flash, but the cyborg rights itself just as quickly.

I stuff the hammer into the side of my boot and bend down to take Cass's hands. Her nail beds are bloody, ripped away from scratching at the sidewalk.

"Sia, help me," she begs.

The cyborg pulls her again, yanking her hands from my grip. She screams my name, over and over.

I leap forward and hold onto her again. Mace and Pax arrive by my side and each take one of Cass's arms.

"Hold on," Pax says. "You're going to be all right."

The three of us tug hard, pulling her away from the machine. The skin around the cyborg's fingers tears as we pull. I watch it shred thick ribbons of skin before Cass's blood gushes out and coats her leg. She screams in spine-chilling agony, and her hands slip out of mine.

The machine grabs her other leg and I know it's over.

I retch and close my eyes. Then I feel Mace guiding me away from Cass, who's beyond our help. Pax stays to finish the machine. Cass's cries rattle my whole body, even my teeth. Then the noise abruptly ends.

The next road is quieter and we regroup there. It takes me a moment to realize that it's Kyra's street. My breath catches mid-inhale. The street is completely ruined.

My eyes are burning. I can see Kyra's house is destroyed before I even get near it. The door is ripped from its hinges, bricks are crumbled around the doorframe. Swallowing the sickening feeling that's raging in my throat, I approach the house.

"It's Kyra's house," Dad says.

I nod. "Just wait here a minute," I say, then dash inside before any of them can stop me.

Stepping into the entryway, my feet crunch beneath me, startling me in the powerful silence that's taken the house. I look down and see, shattered on the floor, Kyra's mom's china plates. Mrs. Foxe collected dozens of them and I wince each time the china crunches beneath my feet.

I round the first corner into the living room. There's a hole ripped out of the floor that I almost fall through. I edge away from it and then I look down.

I'm struck so hard with shock that I almost fall in the hole again. There's a single light bulb on a wire swinging back and forth down there. It no longer works, but the motion makes me dizzy. Below it are the torn-up bodies of the Foxe family.

The nausea in my stomach stirs fiercely and painfully. The Foxes are inside their basement, pillows and sleeping bags on the floor. The shelves on the walls are filled with food, along with entertainment for a long stay. *They thought they could hide.*

I back up and, somehow, find my way out onto the street.

Mace is waiting for me by the front door. "Did you find them?" he asks.

"Yes," I say numbly. "They're all dead."

I turn and throw up right there on the street. Mace rubs my back until the sickness ebbs. It calms, but doesn't go away. I start to wonder whether it ever will after all I've seen.

We've been in one place too long and have to keep moving. We walk in silence beside destroyed homes. No one seems to quite know what to say. I assume everyone's battling with their own thoughts, their own worries, their own fears. We're so unprepared. All that training—all that planning—and for what? For the machines to come early and half-destroy the sector before we can even gather together to help save everyone?

I still feel sick, unbearably so, remembering the bullet lodging itself in Miles's skull, Cass's screams as her skin tore, the Foxes' scattered body parts.

"Sia, are you all right?" Dad says, pressing his hand firmly on my shoulder. I nod, slipping my shoulder from under the weight of his hand. I know we have to keep going, and I know that I can. There's no time for tears and mourning. We're fighting for our lives, and I won't let what we've seen—what I've seen—keep us from our goal.

I feel Dad watching me as I lift up my head before turning back to the rest of the group. "We should get people off the streets and away from the cameras. That was the original plan. Let's get it done." I pull the hammer from my boot, feeling the weight of it in my hand again.

People from the sector are running in all directions toward us.

Dad, Mace, and I wait at the bottom of the hill and lead them up. Those in our group and their relatives already knew the plan we'd made for Day Zero; others we told as we ran through the streets. Some are slower than others— some injured, some old, some carrying children.

Pax and Remy are at the fence, helping people through. It's not long until the cyborgs will make their way here, too. At least the fence might slow them down a bit.

The commotion in the rest of the sector sounds distant now, even though it isn't far away at all. Here, it still feels almost calm. Nothing but bugs disturbs the long grass and patches of weeds around the lake. Nothing but people flee up the hill. No machines, no blood, no fire. *Yet.*

Then something in the long grass stirs.

"There's one here," I say, sure of it.

The second the words leave my lips, a cyborg bursts from the bushes. It charges at us, hands outstretched, eyes dark and powerful. The people behind us scream and move faster toward the hill. Dad turns to help them, hurrying them through the bushes and away from the cyborg.

Then Mace breaks into a run, heading straight for it.

"Mace! No!" I scream.

I hurry to catch up with him as the two bodies, metal and flesh, grow closer. The cyborg is beside the lake now. Mace picks up his pace, running at a slight angle. I know what he's going to do.

I'm just behind him, but he doesn't seem to notice.

Once he's close enough to the machine, he slows, stops, and lifts his leg to kick it into the water. The machine launches itself at Mace. I panic, afraid that it will grab Mace's leg as images of Cass flash before my eyes. I push Mace out of the way, and the machine catches me instead.

It is already falling backward by the time it grabs hold of me. Mace's foot connected with the machine's middle before I pushed him, but metal fingertips tear through my jacket and pull me down, too.

I don't have time to suck in any air and hitting the surface of the lake forces more oxygen from my lungs. The black water swallows me, filling my mouth, my ears, my nose. I kick my legs, but it's no use. I can't swim, and my jacket's still twisted around the cyborg's hand.

I sink, down, down, down.

All the while, the machine twitches like it's malfunctioning. Each spasm scratches my arm. I scream. My throat burns but no sound comes out, only bubbles.

A second splash rocks the surface above, then everything vanishes.

Mace's face is the first thing I see.

I'm coughing and spluttering, gulping greedily for air. My lungs sting with each breath, like I'm inhaling wasps. Mace is leaning over me. His hair is stuck down on his head and little droplets of water drip from the ends. My dad strokes my wet hair back from my face, his expression pained.

"Sia, I'm so sorry," Mace says.

I shake my head. "It wasn't your fault," I say between gasps.

We need to go, so Mace helps me to my feet. Dad walks ahead, leading the way up the hill. There's no time for moving slowly. No time for tripping on the uneven ground. No time for limbs tangling in the overgrown bushes.

At the top, I sit down to catch more breath, and Mace and Pax lower themselves onto the grass on either side of me. There are people everywhere, most clustered together in groups. Some of the badly injured lie on their backs while others gather around them, trying to help. It's dark without any artificial light down in the sector, but blazing fires illuminate what the streetlights do not. Dark smoke covers some areas. In others, I can see people and machines, running, struggling, fighting. I turn away from the terror below, from the ones left behind.

Mace's hip bumps against mine as he shimmies closer. With his hand, he traces lazy circles at the bottom of my back. His touch sparks against my skin, even now.

It's only a short rest. After a couple of minutes we're on our feet again. Pax, Remy, Mace, and I spread out on look-out while Dad tries to organize the people on the hill who can fight. Nobody really knows what to do; it's little more than organized chaos. There are only a handful of people here from the high school meetings. *This is not how things were supposed to be.*

Mace and I walk partway down the hill together to the chain link fence. I stop dead in my tracks. Cyborgs are gathered, pressed up against the fence, breaking it away with little effort. They'll be through in no time.

"We have to warn the others that they're here," I say, turning and rushing back up the hill.

We run, bursting through the bushes and back into the clearing.

"They're here!" Remy yells. "We saw a whole group of them breaking through the fence."

"How many are there?" Dad asks.

"Too many for the five of us," Pax says, shoulders sinking.

Silence. We all look gravely at one another. Finally Dad says, "It's okay. We can do this. We have weapons. We've taken some of them out already. We can do it, I know we can."

No one speaks.

Dad continues, "Don't give up yet. We've still got some fight in us, right?"

"Yeah," Mace says, taking my hand in his. "But there are so many—"

"That's not going to stop us," Dad says. "We've trained hard for this. We can take them."

"What about the other people here? Are they going to help us?" I ask.

Dad looks behind him at the group. "As much as they can," he says.

We stand together, waiting for the cyborgs. I'm convinced that this is the end, my stomach bubbling with nervous energy.

I hear a crash and shortly afterward I see the first machine step out of the bushes. I tense, squeezing the hammer tightly to my chest. The first is followed by another, and another. I stop counting after eight break out into the clearing, and begin to focus on how to take them down.

I urge my feet to move and head for the nearest machine. As it grabs for me, I dive sideways and skirt around it. Once I'm behind, I swing my hammer at the back of its skull. But the cyborg spins around too quickly and I miss.

I jump out of the way of its arms when it goes for me again. Then Dad gets too close, occupied with another cyborg, and he attracts the attention of mine.

"Dad, watch out!" I scream.

He turns in time to fling himself out of the way. I get close, trying to draw the machine's attention back to me, but I'm no match for Dad's fierce energy right now. His life force is pumping out of him.

I plunge the hammer down behind the machine's neck, searching for wires to rip out of its head, but the cyborg won't stay still for long enough, and I lose my hold on the hammer's handle.

I watch in horror as the cyborg latches onto Dad's arm, slicing open his skin. Its fingers are deep enough to brush against bone and it clamps down tighter.

I throw myself at it and yank the hammer out of its neck. It twitches but doesn't slow. *Come on.* It reaches for Dad's waist with its other hand. Abandoning the hammer, I wrap my hands around the cyborg's upper arm and pull back. Its strength is much greater than mine and I don't know how long I can hold on before it breaks away from me.

"Sia, don't," Dad says, his voice strained with pain.

"I'm not letting it have you, Dad."

His next words come hurriedly but none of them register. All I hear is the grunt that bursts from my lips and a crunching sound. All I smell is metal and blood. All I taste is copper and bitterness. All I feel is a burning pain in my shoulders.

All I see is two metal hands, and ten metal fingers, buried deep in my skin.

I don't think I scream. I'm not sure I make any noise at all. My breath leaves me, and the pain flares. The machine's knifelike fingers dig deeper into my shoulders, and my back collides with its cold, solid chest, pinning me to it.

I can hear my name being shouted. The voices blend together in a chorus of panic. Then I hear something else, something distant yet familiar.

I scan the dark sky and see a bright light above the Rough. The sound is an aircraft—the New Worlders must be coming to collect the machines. *But we're not dead*, I think. *Yet.*

The cyborg's fingers fly out of my flesh and I crumple to the ground at its feet. Beside me, Dad swears in anguish as the other machine releases him, too. It seems as though all of the machines have stopped moving.

The wind grows stronger as the aircraft approaches and stops, hovering above us. My T-shirt is sticky with blood and I can't lift myself off the ground. I see Mace just as everything goes black.

When I open my eyes, I'm on the aircraft, leaning against Mace's chest. He twirls a lock of my hair around his finger absently. I look down and see that my injuries have been bandaged.

"What's happening? Where are we going?" I say, wincing as I try to sit up. Mace steadies me.

Dad, Remy, and Pax are sitting opposite us. Remy's wrapping and cleaning Dad's arm wound. Blood drenches the fabric and Remy applies more pressure. Dad grits his teeth while Remy works.

"It's all right, Sia," Mace says. "We're safe."

I glance behind me at people sitting on metal chairs, and lower my voice. "Did the New World come for us?" I whisper. "Mace, they'll kill us when we land. We aren't safe here with them."

I hear a gasp behind me and whirl around.

"I'm offended," I hear Finn say.

"Finn?"

"That's right," he says, smiling. "You sure gave those machines the run around."

"What—?" I shake my head. "What's going on?"

"We came for you guys before we tear down the New World. Didn't think you'd want to miss out on something like that."

"*You* stopped the machines?"

"Yep. With this baby," he says, spinning a small device around in his hand. "I stole it from the labs. Emergency shut down."

I breathe. "Finn, you saved our lives."

"Yep," he says. "And not for the first time." He winks at me.

"We're not out of the deep end yet," I say. "There's still plenty of time for things to go wrong. What's your plan after we land?"

"Something along the lines of guns and fire. I'll explain more when we get there," Finn says.

"That's fine. But I want Damien," I say, then look at Dad. His eyes are fierce and he nods once. "You can destroy the New World. Let us destroy Damien Hoist."

I stare at Finn, watching his reaction, waiting for his response. He takes his time before saying, "Fine. But I won't be far behind you. You get a head start, that's all."

I lean back against Mace and rest. I figure this is the most downtime I'll get. Before all the fighting and all the chaos and all the pain starts again. Mace's arms tighten around my waist.

I think about Damien and everything he's done. Every life he's taken—including my mom's, Kyra's, Lilly's. So much destruction, so much hate, so much pain. I want him to experience that. I want him to know what it feels like. And I want to be there when he does.

The aircraft rattles as we travel head first into a new battle.

We land in the New World.

We're on top of the main building, the same place where I boarded the aircraft to escape only five days ago. There are more people waiting for us up here, all rebels Finn says. There are too many to count before Finn starts shouting orders. He's sending one group to the residential area. A fire will start up top. He tells a group of rebels to get people out, but not to waste any time on those who refuse to leave. I'm uneasy that citizens might be hurt or even killed—a lot of them came here because their only other option was death. I raise my hand in the air. Finn stops and cocks his head to the side. "Sia?"

I clear my throat. "You're not going to kill any citizens, are you?"

Finn smirks. "No. Not unless they get in the way."

"But they're innocent."

"Not all of them."

"But—"

"Let me worry about that part of the plan, Sia," he says, cutting me off. He rubs his forehead. "Team one, you're up. Get people to move down through the city as quickly as possible, then light the fires. We don't want to give the New Worlders enough time to react before they spread."

Team one assembles and exits through the red door with the yellow number.

"Team two, move fast down to commercial. Wait for team one to join you, then light the fires there."

Team two groups and heads to their position.

Finn's smile widens. "The rest of us, we'll look for New Worlders. Take out the guards in particular. You all ready to bring this place down?"

People are cheering around me, but I'm not. Bringing the machines down was one thing, but now we're talking about people. How do we differentiate the good from the bad?

Finn claps his hands. "Let's go, let's go."

Bodies disappear through the red door, and Dad, Remy, Mace, Pax, and I are left standing on the rooftop.

"Let's find Damien," I say.

"Then we kill him. In front of as many people as possible," Dad adds.

I hesitate for a moment. *Kill?* Is that what I want? Do I want Damien dead for everything he's done? I want him to suffer—to realize the pain he has caused so many people. Anger sparks inside. *He deserves it*, I think as I lead the others through the red door.

Since I'm the only one familiar with the New World, I lead the way down the concrete stairs. It's much easier running down them, but my heart still thrashes in my chest and pain stabs my shoulders with each heavy step. I can already hear shouting and chaos from different levels as we pass the red doors.

We make our way down to Level 3 and into the main control room. Some workers look up from their desks. Dad, Remy, and Mace hold up their guns and then panic erupts. Some try to run, and we let them go. Some hide under their desks. Some raise their hands above their heads and stay where they are.

Only moments pass before the alarms screech to life. It's a different alarm from the last time. This sound is more of a long wailing siren—a slow *whoop*—rather than I fast *beep*.

"What does that sound mean?" I say to the worker at the desk closest to me.

"E-evacuation."

"Then, go," I say. "Get out, all of you!"

"Move!" Dad shouts.

Some are hesitant at first, but eventually everyone is moving and heading toward the exit. We continue across the room as it clears. A wall of television screens displays our sector. On some screens, you can't see anything because of the smoke. On others, there are machines fallen or standing as still as statues in the streets, as if frozen. There are bodies and rubble and fire everywhere.

"This way," I say, heading toward the only corridor I haven't been along that branches from this room.

We climb a dark wood and red carpet staircase, a total contrast to everything else I've seen of the New World. The carpet softens our footsteps, making our approach virtually silent. When we reach the top, the corridor branches off to one side and we hear voices around the corner. I hold out my hand, a signal to stop, and peer around the corner.

"Two guards are coming our way," I say. Dad and Remy aim their guns and round the corner before I have chance to say another word. I stare wide-eyed at Mace, but he shakes his head and holds a finger over his lips.

The alarms still blare, the sound splitting my skull in half. Then one, two, three, four, five gunshots rattle in the corridor, overpowering the sound of the alarms.

"This'll draw too much attention to us," I say.

"Finn's teams will be getting all the attention. Don't worry," Mace says.

"Clear," Dad calls. We round the corner. Two guards are face-down on the floor. "Take his gun, Sia," Dad says, jabbing one of the guards with the end of his boot. "You take the other, Pax."

The double doors are made of dark wood, too, and contain a gold plaque that reads Damien Hoist.

The doors have no handles, but some kind of electronic device in the middle instead. I don't understand how it works, and by the looks on the faces of everyone else, they have no idea either.

Dad stuffs his gun into the belt of his jeans and kneels to examine the contraption more closely.

"Maybe you need a swipe card," I say. "That's what they use down in the labs." Dad ignores me, using both hands to pull at it. Tilting his head to the ceiling, he looks inside the small hole at the bottom with one eye closed.

Meanwhile, I walk back over to the guards and search their pockets for an access card, but find nothing.

I return to find Dad sticking his finger inside the hole underneath the device. A bright green light shines out. He jerks his finger out and stands up quickly, pulling his gun from his belt and aiming at the machine. "What *was* that?"

I remember the electronic device I used with Lilly to get here and it clicks. I know what it is.

"It's a scanner!" I say. "To gain access to the room, you must scan a finger or thumb to unlock the door." Dad sticks his finger back inside, but I stop him. "Not you! It needs to be someone who's authorized to enter."

"None of us are."

I jerk my head toward the guards. "They might be."

The five of us heave one of the guards off the floor and drag him over to the door. He's heavy, so it isn't easy. I have hold of one of his huge arms and can feel the muscles beneath his black sweater.

Once we reach the door, Remy lifts the guard's hand to the machine and jams his finger inside. It lights up green again. The light moves slowly down his finger, then back up again before turning off.

Nothing happens.

Sighing, Remy twists the guard's wrist around and it cracks loudly. He then thrusts the guard's thumb into the machine and the light appears again. This time, when the light turns off and Remy ejects the guard's thumb, there's a small click as the door unlocks. Remy, Pax, and Mace roll the guard to the side. Then we ready ourselves to enter Damien's office.

We push through the doors, guns ready, but no one's inside. Dad growls and turns a chair over. "Where *is* he?"

I'm not surprised to find the office empty. There's another door open on the opposite wall. Damien probably left the second the evacuation alarms started blaring.

Dad kicks the far door open wider and leads the way through, with his gun aimed ahead of him. The corridor is bare, minimal. It echoes as Dad steps inside.

I take an extra moment to scan the office before following the others down the corridor. They can't have gone far. Damien can't have escaped, he just *can't*. The alarms haven't been sounding for that long. He must only have a short head start.

Mace shouts back, hurrying me. I run for the doors, but before I get there, a boy slides out of hiding and slams the door shut before I can run through.

I yelp and stagger back. He locks it from the inside. Heavy golden locks slide down at the bottom and top of the door. As my eyes adjust, I recognize the boy from the day I was here. He sat beside me in the cafeteria. He spoke to me in the labs. Cain Hoist.

"W-where did you—?" I stammer. Then I see Damien emerge from hiding.

I shake my head and take another step back. I hear Mace banging against the door on the other side.

"So, this is the girl who's caused us so much trouble," Damien says smoothly.

I pull the gun from my pocket and aim at him. He laughs. "Now, now. There's no need for that."

I feel cold metal on my scalp. "Drop it," Cain whispers. I'm annoyed at my own stupidity. I focused everything on Damien and let Cain sneak behind me and get the upper hand. I drop my weapon, and he picks it up.

Damien sits at his desk. Cain stays standing, watching me. I glare at him.

"What are you both still doing here?"

"We were preparing to leave as you shot our guards outside the door. We opened the escape route and hid so you'd think we'd gone that way."

"Why didn't you—?"

"I'll ask the questions," he says, nodding to Cain. Cain smacks the gun against my skull. I squeeze my eyes shut. Open, shut, open, shut. The whole room spins. "So," Damien says, clasping his hands together. "Let's hear it."

"Hear what?"

"Your problem."

I snort. "My problem? You mean, with you?" He nods. "Apart from killing hundreds of people who don't meet the standards of your 'vision'?"

Damien frowns. "The old sectors, and the people living in them, must be gone for the New World to move forward," he says blandly. I turn around when I hear shots on the other side of the door, but Damien and Cain don't even glance in that direction.

"That doesn't make sense," I say, looking back at him. "Why can't you just let us go? If you aren't happy to have us here in the New World, then why not take the walls down and let us out?"

He laughs. "Then we wouldn't have control over any of you."

"So?"

"If we let everyone go we wouldn't be able to keep tabs on them, we wouldn't know where everyone was. Then what would happen? The people would target us, fight against the New World because they weren't allowed in. It wouldn't be in our best interest to simply let people go. It'd be too much of a liability."

"Then why not just let the sectors stay as they are? Continue with the New World development, but leave those you don't want back in the old sectors, carrying on with their lives?"

"Do you really think you'd be able to carry on without us? We provide you with everything. You'd die if we abandoned you. We're just . . . speeding along the process."

"You really believe that what you're doing is acceptable, is humane?"

Damien shrugs. His wicked smile makes me shiver. "I don't know what you think you're going to achieve by coming here, but I can tell you that you won't get far."

I hear the sound of wood chipping, cracking. I look back at the door.

"They won't get in," Damien says.

"They will," I reply.

Damien's face in unreadable, but I must have rattled him because he stands up and tells Cain to get ready to leave.

"It seems there were a few traitors among us," Damien says, righting his suit jacket.

"More than a few," I say.

"None of this matters, anyway. We can come back from this. You can't."

Just then the door crashes open and Pax and Mace stagger in, followed by Dad and Remy. Damien jumps, and Cain aims his gun and shoots at the four of them. I throw my arms around his body, tackling him to the ground and pounding my fist into his face. Pinning him down with my legs, I wrap my hands around his throat. "Don't move," I bark, and he attempts to laugh.

I look up to see Mace and Dad detaining Damien, holding a gun to his head. Remy's pointing his gun at Damien as well. Pax is sitting on the desk with his hand on his shoulder, blood seeping out between his fingers. I grit my teeth against the throbbing of the fresh wounds in my shoulder and clamp down harder on Cain's throat.

"We need to get downstairs," Dad says. "Pax, are you all right to move?" Pax nods, cringing at the pain from his wound. "All right, let's go."

As I ease my weight off Cain's body, he twists around and elbows me in the face. The blow to my nose, still tender from my last visit to the New World, causes instant agony. The pain is unimaginable as the cartilage clicks. I gasp for air, feeling like I'm going to throw up. Gunshots pass overhead as the others aim for Cain as he runs for the exit. I lift my own gun and pull the trigger. I see the bullet clip Cain's arm. But that's not enough.

"After him!" I shout.

Mace and Remy make chase as I shove myself back up to my feet. I hold my nose with my free hand and follow them down the escape corridor. It's a concrete tunnel. Bulbs light the way. My footsteps echo as my boots slap against the hard floor. My nose and my shoulders feel as if they are on fire.

I keep going until I find Mace and Remy retreating toward me, without Cain. "Where is he?" I ask.

"He more or less vanished," Mace says. I growl in frustration. He's gone, and there's nothing I can do about it.

"He's Damien's son. We better be quick before he tells someone we have his dad," I say, breaking into a run.

The three of us rush back to Damien's office. Pax is sitting on a chair looking pale, his hand pressed against his wound and covered in blood.

"Cain got away," I say, breathless. "We need to hurry."

I lead the way out of the office and back down the carpeted staircase. Dad follows, holding his gun against Damien's back. Damien's suit is ruffled, his shirt hanging loose, his blazer buttons strained with his heavy breathing.

The main room is cleared of workers. The alarms have stopped, but I can still hear the chaos roaring through the building. I wonder how long it'll take for the fire to reach us down here.

I guide them to the room where they air the Reports. If Dad wants the most people to witness Damien's execution, this is as public as it gets.

Glass doors lead into a smaller room that's painted floor-to-ceiling in white. There's a single camera pointed at an ever-changing backdrop, and a television screen beside it. The other side of the room holds a desk with several computers and headsets.

Pax turns on the television and camera, then Remy and Dad position Damien in front of the lens. The camera starts recording. We're on air. I give them the thumbs up. *Go.*

"We're here in the New World with Damien Hoist," Dad says, staring straight into the camera. "As you know, this man created this place and is the cause for all of your suffering. Today, our sector was attacked by the machines, and we survived."

Damien closes his eyes. Hopeless. He's got no choice but to give up—exactly the way he made every person left in the sectors feel right before he sent the cyborgs in to slaughter them. Death almost seems too kind for Damien now.

Dad continues, "We are airing this Report to tell you that you will survive, too. There will be no more attacks. This picking and choosing of who lives and who dies ends today."

He stops speaking, turns, and nods at Remy. Dad looks to me for a split second, then raises his gun and fires.

Silence follows. Dad releases Damien's body, allowing it to fall heavily to the ground. *It's over*, I think. *Damien's gone.*

Then the glass doors beside us shatter into a million pieces.

I duck and cover my face, keeping low and moving toward the wall.

The gunfire stops and the moments that follow are painfully silent—all I hear is my own ragged breath. Mace crawls over to me and positions himself in front of me, protecting me, but I don't want him to. I don't want Mace to shield my body with his own.

"Show yourselves, traitors."

More silence.

Then the air erupts with gunfire once again, but it's not aimed at us this time. I wish I could see what's happening in the main room.

New World guards stumble into our room, out of the chaos. Mace shoots one man in the leg and he falls to his knees. The New Worlder raises his gun, aims at Mace. I

241

lift my gun and shoot him in the chest. His body hits the ground.

A bullet whizzes by my head, burying itself in the wall behind me. Someone kills the shooter, I don't know who. The small room is packed with us and guards and Finn's rebels and I don't know who to aim for anymore.

I'm still on the ground. As more people pile into the room, I worry it's not the safest place. I feel like I'll die if I stand up or I'll die if I stay here.

I decide to stand. Crouching behind a desk, I raise my gun and aim for the figures wearing black. I am only assuming they're the New Worlders, so I don't shoot unless I have to. And when one turns and aims at me, I pull the trigger and the next thing I know, he's on the ground, a hole in his head leaking red. I look away.

I'm so far from the door I have no hope of getting out without being hurt or killed. And what's outside isn't much safer. The fighting seems to have moved to this floor while the upper levels burn, and no one's getting out until one side has won. I hope it's ours. It has to be ours.

Mace's body presses against my left side suddenly, reassuring. I have no idea where my dad, Remy, and Pax are—no idea if they're still in the room or if they're even still alive. It kills me not knowing. I just want this to be over.

The room starts to clear. The floor is littered with bodies of the injured and dead. I can't stay here any longer, waiting, wondering.

"Mace, let's go," I say, moving to the edge of the desk.

He takes my hand. "I'll go first."

He steps out from behind the desk before I can protest. I follow him.

A guard turns, aims, but I get him first. I hear another shot, close, and a grunt behind me. I turn and find a New Worlder at my feet, then glance back to see Finn smiling with his gun pointed my way.

"That's three times now," Finn shouts, holding up three fingers. "Three times I've saved your life, if anyone's keeping count."

I nod my thanks and keep moving toward the exit. My heart's bouncing in my chest as I scan the room for Dad. The small number of New Worlders who are left abandon the fight, give up their weapons, and surrender as they realize how much the rebels outnumber them now.

More people pile into the camera room, guns poised. I raise mine, too.

"Hold your fire," Finn shouts, and I can breathe again. They're rebels. There are only rebels left standing. We won. *We won!* "I said I'd only give you guys a head start. I see you made the most of it." He nods at Damien's body. "Let's get out of here before this place collapses."

I look for Dad before we leave, but he isn't among the living or the dead. I start to panic. *Maybe he got out,* I think. *But what if he didn't?*

We move with Finn and his team to the main entrance. The power cuts, and we run down unmoving escalators. We stop outside and see that the blue blaze of the laser gates is off, too, so we continue out of the building and toward the aircrafts.

I take one last look behind me, at the New World, which is now lit up with fire. Flames lick the sky and black clouds fill the air. Mace slips his arms around my waist from behind and rests his head on my shoulder. "Are you ready to go home?" he says, his breath tickling my neck.

I scan the tarmac, between the aircrafts, and through the groups of people. I spot my dad and Remy, holding Pax between them. They're standing beside an aircraft, scanning the crowds of people that pour from the entrance.

"Yes," I say, smiling.

As Mace goes to support Pax, Dad rushes over and hugs me fiercely. He kisses my hair and holds tight. It hurts—my body hurts so much—but I can't let go.

"Where were you?" he asks me over and over, seemingly overwhelmed with relief. I can't find the words. I thought he might be gone, too. It was all too much, too quick, too frightening. But we're all right now. We're together. We're okay.

On the aircraft, I curl up next to Mace as we take off into the smoky sky and head for home.

The sector is ruined.

Many of the buildings are no longer standing. The streets are blackened with soot. The last of the fires are crackling and dying down. Bodies litter the streets, and blood marks every surface. Machines stand like metal sculptures.

How can I live here now?

"Don't worry," Dad says, as if reading my mind. He squeezes my hand. "We'll get there in time."

The other aircrafts don't stop with us—they head on to other sectors to start taking down the walls. Finn told me he'd see me again as he headed off to help, but I don't know how soon that'll be.

Mace and I walk behind Dad, Remy, and Pax to Miles's house. It feels wrong going back there now that he's dead. But, then again, most people we know are now dead. I start to wonder how many must have died today, added to the hundreds that have died leading up to it—at the hands of machines, hit by a bullet, caught in flames, or crushed beneath rubble. Suicide. So many. So, so many. I can't even grasp it all.

Miles's house is damaged—a few broken windows and the hole in the wall—but it's not too bad. I guess there had been no one inside to draw the machines back to it. Remy and Pax leave to go search for their own families. I hope more than anything that they are safe.

Inside, the house is cold and quiet. Dad raids the kitchen for what little food is left. I wonder how we'll survive now, without the authorities providing for us.

We'll get there in time.

0 DAYS

Dull evening light streaks into the living room, coming through the holes in the wall.

I should be dead now but I'm not.

The New World was destroyed, not me.

The metal walls surrounding the sector will be taken down, panel by panel. We finally have our freedom.

We are the first sector with survivors, and the last sector to suffer such a terrible fate. We ended it.

I stand and stretch, wondering how long I was out for. I'm filthy from yesterday. My clothes are crusted with dry dirt and blood, and my hair smells like smoke. I force myself to stand and go upstairs to the bathroom. My bottle of water is still on the counter, half-full, and I step into the shower with it and a bar of soap.

I drain my bottle, washing the blood and dirt off my body as best I can.

When I'm done, I grab a towel and wrap it around myself, then examine my body for cuts and bruises in the bathroom mirror. There are lots of tiny scrapes and grazes, mainly on my arms and hands, and multiple gashes on my cheekbones. My nose particularly stands out—the skin around it is raised and swollen, surrounded by a dark-purple bruise. I press my fingers to it and wince. Both my knees are bruised, and a few faded yellow ones are dotted across my arms and chest.

I pull back the bandages that cover my shoulders and find ten punctures.

"Those bandages will need changing," Mace says, coming into view behind me in the mirror.

He envelops me in a hug. I'm suddenly very conscious that all I'm wearing is a towel. He kisses my neck and whispers into my ear. "I have something for you. In your room."

He takes a step back from me and steps toward the door. "Wait," I say, spinning around and taking his arm. "Everything isn't going to just get better now, is it?"

Mace puts his hands on my hips and traces lazy circles with his finger on one side. "Honestly? I don't know."

"We were the ones on camera," I say. "We're the face of this. Everyone knows what we did, and not everyone is going to support it. And Cain. Cain got away, and we killed his dad. If that was me, I . . . I don't know what I'd do. Damien had to have planned for his demise. What if Cain was his second-in-command? That means we didn't take down the entire New World—at least not while Cain might still be out there, along with the others who helped build it."

"Save it for another day, Sia," Mace says, smiling. "We've got time. Time we didn't have before. Enjoy it, at least for a little bit."

I purse my lips.

"Just for today, then," he says.

I nod and slip the T-shirt he gave to me over my head, letting it fall down to my knees and pull on my jeans. I follow him to the bedroom.

On the desk is a bunch of flowers in a tall mug. My breath catches when I see them. "What? How?" I say. My hands shake as I reach for them, running my fingers over their smooth, silky petals, and inhaling their sweet scent.

"Some of the wall panels are already down. We're free, Sia."

Releasing the flower petals, I run down the stairs and out through the front door, barefoot. I stop in the middle of the road and gaze down the street.

Where the road had once come to an end is no longer a sky-high metal wall, but endless lands full of colorful, beautiful life.

Mace joins me in the street, handing my boots to me. I slip them on and run for the border.

My heart skips when I take that first step from gray pavement to soft earth.

I keep running until I'm under the trees; I touch their trunks and feel the rough bark beneath my fingers for the first time. This is what I wanted.

This is all I wanted.

I'm finally free.

Acknowledgments

Thank you to my agent Isabel Atherton and editors Julie Matysik and Nicole Frail, for loving this book as much as I do. And to the wonderful team at Sky Pony Press for everything you've done in bringing this book together.

To fellow Sky Pony author Rose Mannering, for going along this path first and turning back to tell me what's up ahead.

To A. G. Howard and Claire Merle for your guidance before and after. I'll always consider you both a part of my journey.

A special thank you to Emma Pass for being my first reader, for your passion toward this book, and for the advice you have given to me.

The lovely authors, readers, and bloggers on Twitter, who have become my friends, which includes the Author Allsorts, who I must also thank for insightful blog posts and great teamwork.

My good friend (and boss!) Scharlotte Walsh, for your understanding and enthusiasm. You made sure I had the time to write this book and always asked how things were going with it. And many thanks to other friends and colleagues who've been incredibly supportive.

To my furry assistant Freddie, for keeping me company. And much love to my family and Andy, for encouragement and support the whole way and for believing in me at times when I didn't even believe in myself.

ABOUT THE AUTHOR

Kate Ormand is the author of circus–shapeshifting adventure *The Wanderers* and the sequel, *The Pack*. She graduated from university with a degree in fine art painting. There, she discovered her love of reading YA books, prompting her to try a new creative angle and experiment with writing. Kate also writes children's picture books under the name Kate Louise. She lives in Cheshire, England, with her family, her partner, and a cocker spaniel named Freddie.

The Wanderers
by Kate Ormand

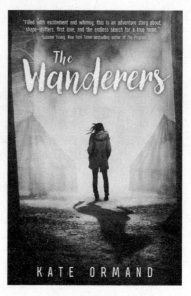

"An utterly captivating big-top world filled with shape-shifters and dark secrets. I devoured this book! It was unlike anything I've ever read." —Amy Christine Parker, author of *Gated and Astray*

Flo lives an eccentric life—she travels with a popular circus in which the main acts star orphaned children with secret shape-shifting abilities. Once Flo turns sixteen, she must perform, but she's not ready. While practicing jumping a flaming hurdle in a clearing beside the circus, she spots a dark figure in the trees and fears he saw her shift. The news sends the circus into a panic.

In Flo's world, shifters are unknown to humans with the exception of a secret organization. They send some shifters to labs for observation and testing—testing they don't often survive—and deem others useless, a danger to society, and eliminate them. To avoid discovery, shifters travel in packs, constantly moving and keeping themselves hidden. Up until now, the circus was the perfect disguise.

Flo manages to flee the torched circus grounds with Jett, the bear shifter who loves her; the annoying elephant triplets; and a bratty tiger named Pru. Together they begin a new journey, alone in a world they don't understand and don't know how to navigate. On the run, they unravel secrets and lies that surround the circus and their lives—secrets and lies that all point to the unthinkable: Have they been betrayed by the people they trusted most?

$8.99 Paperback ISBN 978-1-5107-1535-6

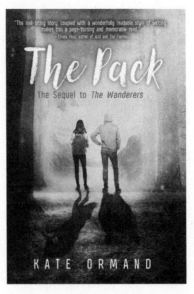